ε {

Sincere gratitude...

THE SOUNDS
OF SILENCE

CHARLES MICHAEL LANDRY

DEDICATION

This book is dedicated to my wife to die for, Dianne, my sons Daniel and Justin and my daughter and angel, Tayla, without whom my life would be an empty book...

CONTENTS

ACKNOWLEDGMENTS

I would like to thank the greater Landry family and every one of my friends from all over the world for supporting my efforts in creating this work and everything else I do in life including music. In particular, I would like to thank my editors: my soul brother Joe F Hanley, his daughter Jenn Knight, my big sister Donna Giuliana and our close friend Debbie Gallagher. I would also like to thank my proof reading volunteers: Glen Arlequeeuw, Joanne Aleo, Diane Mackin, and Kiley Mackin who got so many e-mails from me that they have probably been redirected to the junk mail folder or blocked by now. Special gratitude goes out to Angela Page and Ron Lovely for your guidance in helping me get this idea not only on paper but bringing it to the market. Finally, I would like to thank all of my friends and the people in Seoul Korea. You have inspired me on a very deep level and this book is also dedicated to you.

1. THE DREAM JOB

A single car is stopped at a railroad crossing. The railway gate is down and the bell is sounding but there is no train in sight. A closer look at the car from the opened passenger side window reveals a pile of packages on the seat with exotic names and places on the shipping labels. The boxes are addressed to Hong Kong, Taipei and such, but the box on top which is clearly visible is being shipped to Seoul, South Korea. Nothing else about the address or recipient is recognizable when compared to a US shipping label. It is completely foreign. On the passenger side floor are eight cups of coffee in two cup holders. The driver is a young man named Andrew Trainor. While waiting for the train he has found a moment to rest his eyes and gently slips into a daydream.

He suddenly finds himself peering through the rear window of a house, scouting out the situation inside. A valuable government agent has been kidnapped and is being held in an abandoned house out in the deep woods.

Andrew watches long enough to determine that there are five armed kidnappers inside. He pauses just long enough to whisper, "Its go time." He quietly pulls up the bottom window sash and slips into an empty room. He is as still as the wallpaper hugging the wall until one of the men enters the room. Andrew, who is unarmed, lunges forward toward the man putting his hands over his mouth and violently twists his neck taking him out before he even has a chance to reach for his weapon. With silent steps like a cat, he ambushes one kidnapper after another until there is only a trail of bodies left behind him.

Bursting into the room where our victim is being held, Andrew finds a beautiful woman who still manages to look stunning even after days of being roughed up and tortured. He swiftly cuts the duct tape that binds her, takes her by the hand and silences all of her rapid fire questioning by telling her to just trust him. They race hand in hand out of the back of the house and through the thick woods to a clearing where they wait for a helicopter that is carefully approaching for a landing and clean getaway. The woman takes Andrew by the chin and pulls his gaze her way. He has just saved her life and she cannot stop herself from wanting to kiss him. This quintessential moment feels very familiar to Andrew for he has visualized it happening hundreds of times before. The woman pulls Andrew's face very slowly toward hers as her eyes begin to close and her lips begin to part.

At this point the extremely loud sound of a commuter train with its horn blasting yanks Andrew out of this woman's arms and indeed out of his daydream entirely with the intensity of an electric shock. He is mildly sweating but composes and reorients himself to his environment: the inside of his parked car in front of raising railroad crossing gates. As Andrew glances over at the boxes and coffee, he puts his car back into drive and says to himself in a less enthusiastic tone, "It's go time." The truth of the matter is that Andrew is not a secret agent or the international spy he's always dreamed about. He is "the new guy" at Tilton Global Resources, a Washington based US Government contracting firm. Tilton runs routine tasks around the world for various government agencies including the CIA and is also hired out for some occasional black ops missions; at least this is the rumor running under people's breath in the office. Andrew's "mission" this morning is to deliver packages to UPS on his way into the office and perhaps the most critical and tactical task of the day, pick up everyone's morning coffee. He has been working at Tilton Global for just over a month and although his current role in the company is a bit underwhelming and would never be mistaken as his dream job, at least he knows he has the potential for more important things and is in the right place with his foot in the door.

He makes it to UPS and accomplishes his daily routine of shipping packages. They now know him by his first name and often slip up and call him Andy, a name he passionately hates. He doesn't hesitate to immediately correct them. With the packages now safely on their way, soon he is pulling his ten-year-old car into the company's secure parking garage. He pulls into the only space not taken by a BMW or a Lexus and makes his way into the office with his briefcase in one hand and the hot stash of liquid gold coffee balancing on his other arm.

As Andrew walks into the lobby and makes his way through security, one of the screeners jokes with him, "Where's my coffee?" The young security agent has made the same comment several times over the past few weeks, each time getting the rest of the screeners to join him in taunting Andrew as they all ask about their coffee too. Andrew knows that these guys have way too much time on their hands and are trying to lighten their own mood at his expense. This time Andrew is going to put this jokester in his place. "These highly prized beverages are for an elite group of agents that are critical to the successful functioning of this company. The day I see you take a bunch of files off my desk and process them is the day your name gets added to my coffee list!" Andrew replies. He's on a roll now and continues, "In fact, one day you'll find me with a very big title in this company and I'll personally see that you get promoted to the valet team so you can have the privilege of parking my car and running out to get my coffee." As Andrew walks away holding on to his dignity as carefully as he holds onto the coffee cups, he can hear the young screener shouting over his coworkers laughter, "Don't do me any favors!"

Once Andrew steps off the elevator on the second floor, he is greeted more enthusiastically by his own co-workers. He waltzes his way from cubicle to cubicle dropping off one coffee order after another while correctly identifying out loud each blend and composition with impeccable accuracy. A double mocha latte here, a double barrel espresso shot cappuccino there. When he has called out and delivered the final cup of coffee to the eagerly awaiting staff, he bows as he's given a standing ovation and receives various accolades. The glory of this moment fades after he walks into his cube and finds his in-box stacked twelve inches higher than it was yesterday when he left it. Processing paperwork and correctly filing it is a dirty and potentially dangerous job, Andrew thinks to himself as he sits down at his desk staring at the pile of paper that constituted an entire tree not so long ago. Someone could misplace a file and innocent people could die. Well maybe not die exactly but the folks in his office would at a minimum be very uncomfortable until the file was finally found. He consoles himself by thinking that every secret agent began their career by pushing papers around and learning the ropes until they were tapped by upper management and given a chance to shine. He will follow in their footsteps until he and his worldly talents are discovered by a company executive. "Who is that guy?" the CEO would ask his secretary running behind him with a stack of files. "Get him up to my office right away." Andrew could see himself being escorted to the elevators for that ride to the top floor, the floor not even listed on the elevator buttons and only accessed by a key, fingerprints and eye scan identification. He would walk in as a middle-aged, average adult and would walk out as a human lethal weapon in a tuxedo twirling the keys to his own BMW. However, at the moment, the company printer is out of toner so it's time to spring into action, roll up his sleeves and get his hands covered in toner like a chimney sweep.

Meanwhile, on the thirty-second floor of the same building, a man who also works for Tilton Global is staring at his computer monitors and shaking his head. He is wrestling with his conscience over the position he's been put in again by his own company. They are involving him

5

and his talents in coordinating the secret funding for individual assassins taking on a new dark project. This time the death squad will be working a little closer to home; too close for him to close his eyes to it. The running excuse is that war is war, no matter where the engagement happens to take place. This is just another lucrative job and if they don't do it, another company will in a heartbeat. And when did aspiring political figures who just happen to end up on the wrong side of someone's fence sign up for that war? "If these people want to kill each other off entirely, the world just may end up being a better place," the man concludes with a diminishing conscience. Nevertheless, he is primarily worried about one thing: getting caught. If there is an intensive investigation after these killings and someone just follows the money, the buck stops right at his desk with him still sitting at it.

He decides to follow through with a plan to get hard evidence about the mission onto a company memory stick and smuggle it out of the building in order to have it at his disposal as a safety net. If there is a possibility of him going down, then everyone else is going down with him. But there is a problem with the memory stick however. All USB memory sticks in the building have a security beacon program running in the background that triggers if a stick is plugged into any unauthorized computer inside or outside the building with an unauthorized MAC address. These special memory sticks are sequestered, are not permitted to leave the building and in fact will trigger an alarm if one goes through the building's security system. Although he just wants the evidence on hand and does not plan to plug it into another computer to set off the beacon, it will be incredibly challenging just to get it out of the building.

He has obviously thought this process out in great detail before now. The company has continuously pushed him and other agents into situations that they found hard to swallow. But when you become part of an intelligence war, covert or not, your heart begins to harden and you learn to do what you're told. There is a restroom on the second floor that has a window that can be opened and it is positioned directly above landscaped hedges lining the outside of the building below. The memory stick alone is too light and if the wind catches it, it will be difficult to control its flight path. However, he calculates that if he attaches the USB stick to some keys to create more solid weight, he can drop the key set straight down behind the hedges where he can later retrieve them. He decides he will complete this task tomorrow just after five o'clock when people have left for the day. This will be his only chance.

In the meantime, Andrew has now completed working his regular shift and after saying goodnight to a handful of the crew lagging behind, he makes his way to his car. Traffic is light today and he's home in almost no time at all. He had been invited earlier to join some of the guys for drinks after work at a lounge that was particularly popular with local women but Andrew had remained noncommittal. He knew and they all knew that he wouldn't go, but one day he might just surprise them and show up. Once Andrew gets home and settles down after dinner, he takes out his violin, opens his window, climbs out onto his fire escape overlooking the courtyard below, sits back on some well-worn cushions and begins to play.

The acoustics in the courtyard are hypnotizing since there are three tall walls from the building making it into a quasi-amphitheater. Andrew plays for hours as the elegant sounds of the rich instrument bounce back and forth between the walls introducing long delayed echoes and harmonics. No one in his complex ever complains about his music. Most people keep their windows open or open them wider and take in the free concert as they prepare dinner or go about their business. Andrew's outdoor evening music sessions have become as routine as Sunday morning church bells; also a familiar call in the distance.

Music has held a prominent role in Andrew's life for as long as he could remember. After his father left him and his mother when he was still very young, Andrew had filled the void by becoming the de facto man of the house. He had a very close relationship with his mother and she always encouraged Andrew to stick with his music. It was the glue that held his life together no matter how tough things got. Even years later after losing his mother to cancer, music was there waiting for him during his prolonged grieving process. Music became Andrew's way of conversing with the universe and he always believed in his heart that the universe was out there listening to him, with his mother smiling somewhere in the front row.

The next day Andrew is back at work. Not long after lunch he is asked by his manager to stay a little later this evening to work off some of his overflowing inbox. He has no family of his own at home or even a girlfriend since they would only slow down the life of a secret agent or a world traveling company asset, so he has no plans for the evening and is more than happy to put in some extra time on the clock. Time flies when you're having fun and before Andrew knows it, it's 7 p.m. and time to wrap up for the day. He actually got quite a bit accomplished and put a significant dent in his backlog of work. The building by now is virtually empty as one can easily see from all the open parking spaces in the garage. During the short walk to his car, Andrew finds a small set of keys on the ground. He looks all around the immediate garage area for one of his coworkers or anyone who might know something about the keys, but he is alone. Someone has dropped them obviously, but who? There is no identification on the keys but after picking up and examining the key set, he finds that there is a memory stick on the key ring. Maybe a clue to identifying the owner of the keys and making someone's day can be determined by checking the files on the stick. "It couldn't hurt to simply peek at some of the files to find a name, right?" Andrew tells himself. Some poor fellow employee is probably locked out of his home at this very moment or is just going crazy looking for those keys. He hops into his car, drops the "lost and found" keys into his coffee cup holder in the center console and makes his way home.

Unbeknownst to Andrew, not even an hour prior to his discovering those keys, the man from the thirty-second floor had executed his plan with incredible precision. He then recovered the keys with the USB stick attached outside behind the hedges and placed them in his coat pocket. He then casually made his way up into the garage where he removed the keys from his pocket placing them on the hood of his car, removed his coat and methodically hung it on a coat hanger in the back seat. He then checked his buzzing phone for a few messages as he opened the driver's side door and sat down to start up his keyless new car. After attaching his phone to the car charger, he shifted into drive and immediately drove off. The keys remained on the hood for all of about two seconds before sliding off and falling to the ground. He would not discover that the keys were lost until he arrived home several hours later. He immediately jumped right back in his car and returned in a panic to the company garage only to find no trace of the keys or the memory stick at which point he decisively wished that he was already dead.

2. THE KEY THAT OPENS THE WRONG DOOR

Walking into his apartment, Andrew hangs his coat, drops his briefcase and sets the keys he found on his home office desk before going to the fridge for a cold beer. He has priorities and unwinding is at the top of his list. As he takes his first few sips of beer, the mystery of those keys won't leave him alone. Instead of simply bringing them back in the office in the morning and sending out an email blast about the lost keys, Andrew decides to find the identity of the unfortunate person who lost them and hand deliver the keys himself in a more heroic fashion. It takes seemingly forever for his computer to boot up so he waits patiently. "This poor PC must be crawling with worms and viruses now. It takes longer to boot this stupid computer up every day," he mumbles to himself. Finally he sees his desktop screen and pushes the memory stick still attached to the keys into the USB port. After viewing the contents of the memory stick and seeing that there are hundreds of files to choose from, Andrew randomly opens a file with the acronym title "OFF." The file doesn't open at first but after a few tries, it finally does and Andrew is completely shocked at what he is now staring at. The document is highly classified and identifies a project with a code name, Operation Friendly Fire. As he reads through the material, chills run through his spine and a deep sense of fear begins to set in. "What the hell is this?" Andrew murmurs while barely breathing. Like a tragic automobile accident where cars are mangled and smoking, as much as you don't want to look, you are actually unable to stop yourself from staring at it. This file he is reading outlines a hellish plot where a list of prominent American citizens will be assassinated on US soil by contracted militia snipers. Initially, it is difficult to decipher who is ordering this attack, why these specific people are being targeted and all the players involved but the premise is clear enough. People are going to die and something will need to be done to prevent it. Although Andrew is unaware of it, the virtual beacon software in the USB stick is now broadcasting his location and announcing to interested parties that these top secret files have been compromised. Simultaneously, as Andrew looks at these files in his apartment, a computer system at the Tilton Global security office picks up on the beacon. A flashing warning signal on a computer screen with a GPS locator indicates that an unauthorized individual is accessing classified information. Immediate action will be required to deal with the situation.

"How could this happen?" the night security operations manager yells out to the frenzied staff now scrambling around the room. "This is going to hurt, I can just feel it. Get everyone in here right now. I don't care if you have to drag them out of bed!" Within a few hours' time, a group of company officials and strategists convene in a conference room on one of the upper floors of the building. The senior director who is clearly in charge in the room demands an update. "Tell me everything we know." "The beacon identified the breach at 19 Edgemoor Drive in Bethesda, Maryland," exclaims a computer operator who is rapidly typing away in front of his bank of monitors. "It's the home of one Andrew Trainor, age twenty-nine who's employed at… he works for us. He's one of our own, John." "What is his security clearance? Is he even a threat at all?" asks the director. "Apparently sir, he's an office clerk with no security clearance or authority at all. Just a low level office worker in the documentation department downstairs." "Find out more, damn it! What is he looking at and how did he get these files?" the director demands. "How does a "nobody" end up with information like this that can potentially hang us? Find out who got this information out of the building. Find them and shoot them! Let's reconvene in the morning and try to save our asses. Put an immediate tag on this Andrew Trainor! If he takes a piss, I was to know about it!"

Andrew sits back on his chair at home as thoughts rapidly bombard his brain. His body is experiencing nervous spasms as if preparing to throw up something his body is totally rejecting. Paranoia starts to take hold of him as he quickly closes every curtain and shade in his apartment thinking he is already being watched. He aggressively shuts down his computer and rips the USB stick out only to sit back down and stare at it in total disbelief. "What the hell am I gonna do now? I can't return this to the office. Someone will know I had access to the data." He starts shutting off everything in his house with a plug, strips down in his bedroom and kills the last remaining light as he slowly crawls into bed. "Maybe I'll just put the keys back where I found them," he thinks to himself. He then carefully and systematically traces back his steps in his mind to the security garage. "Was there a camera recording me when I picked up those keys?" he wonders as he tries to recall the location of the dozens of security cameras covering virtually every inch of the facility. He is torn between just throwing the keys and USB stick off the bridge into the river in the morning or dropping them off anonymously in a blank envelope at the offices of the Washington Post. He is also tossing and turning and not sleeping. There is no sleep or peace on the horizon for him right now.

As Andrew wakes up the next morning after worrying himself half to death but eventually to sleep, he becomes painfully aware that it was not all a nightmare. From his bed, he can still see the keys and USB staring right back at him. As he prepares for work, he decides to just keep things to himself and try to act normal until he can figure out what to do. Suddenly the thought of being a spy and carrying around government secrets has lost all of its attraction for him. He feels so nervous that breakfast is out of the question. He realizes that he is so shaky that he also better skip his morning shave to save his skin from imminent danger. He is praying for a way to save himself, wishing he could turn back the clock to the point just before he picked up those damn keys.

At the same time back at Tilton headquarters about thirty floors above Andrew's office, there is an intelligence team in conference. "Gentlemen, you all know why we're here. What do we have?" barks the director. "Trainor never left his apartment last night and didn't make any calls. No Facebook posts or even a tweet out of him," replies one of the officers with an open manila folder in front of him displaying Andrew's picture and various data files about his life. "The files on Operation Friendly Fire, which is currently the only joint project between Tilton and the CIA, were in the hands of only a top level working group including some of the people in this room now. The files themselves are highly encrypted and on a secure server. For reasons unknown to us now, it appears that someone in the group screen captured a few pages from the files putting the captures on a memory stick. Now, as we are all aware, part of our joint CIA security protocol requires Security Beacon USB memory sticks that trigger notification when any computer outside the building attempts to use or read them. Since these special memory sticks are sequestered, it's impossible to get them out of the building, yet somehow this one seems to have slipped through the cracks. As for motivation, perhaps somebody wanted insurance if this project backfires and they get called out." "Surely you must be joking," snapped the director breaking the silence. "Just slipped out? The most secure, encrypted information on the damn planet and someone is allowed to hit a control and print button on a keyboard and walk away with evidence that can lock us all up? Even one of my kids would have thought of that possibility!" No one in the room dares to respond or make eye contact. "OK, get me Trainor's manager on the phone. It's early so try his cellphone. We're in no position to wipe this Andrew Trainor off the map right now but maybe we can push him around the map a bit and get him out of the way."

The meeting adjourns and shortly thereafter the director picks up the phone in his office after his secretary chimes in saying, "We have Andrew Trainor's manager on the line, sir." The director greets the Documentation Department Manager by saying, "We have a little problem, Tom." Tom himself does not have enough security clearance to know anything about the operation so he too must be kept in the dark. After the director gives a detailed explanation of a totally fabricated situation, they then come up with an immediate action plan to send Andrew out for a "field trip" and get him involved in real company business on the front lines. Tom assures the director, "Don't worry. I'm not exactly sure why you want Andrew for this job since he's so new, but I don't think I'll have any problem convincing him to go. I've had many talks with him and he has great aspirations now that he's with us. I'll set everything up and let you know if there are any problems." Andrew's manager hangs up the phone and ponders for a few moments over the logic the company is using in choosing Andrew for this task. He finally shakes his head and walks away giving up on making any sense of the situation. "Why don't they send me? I could use a vacation myself!" he mumbles to himself as he gets into his car for his drive into work. After the company director hangs up the phone on his end, he immediately connects back with his secretary asking her to connect him to their South Korean Intelligence Office insider.

Meanwhile, Andrew's car slowly approaches the company building and he stops long enough to decide whether to turn around and start driving to the Canadian border or man up and walk back into the building. He then gathers up enough courage to pull into the garage, parks in his usual spot and prepares to go into his office. Getting out of his car, he fights the urge to look down at the spot where he found the keys just in case cameras are already focused on him. As he approaches the front door using his back to push it open, he makes it through security with his armload of coffee. He pauses for a minute just outside his office and musters up a forced smile as he goes through his coffee delivery routine. For a moment things are back to normal. He makes his way into his office and as he grimaces at the paper mountain reaching ever greater heights on his desk, his office phone begins ringing. It's his supervisor. "Andrew, you've been chosen to go out in the field and assist in a project. Are you free to travel to South Korea soon? We need you to join a crew in cleaning up a safe house operation that went south?" "Why me?" Andrew asks. "I'm just a paper pusher here. What am I supposed to do?" His supervisor assures him that he is perfect for the job. He's been chosen because no one knows him or has ever seen his face in Seoul therefore he can move about freely without attracting any suspicion. "Go home and pack for the trip. All of your expenses will be paid so this won't cost you a penny. You will be helping us out of a very tight situation so you'll be looking at a pretty nice bonus when you return. By the way, before you go, stop and buy some basic tools, a cordless drill driver and some drill bits. You'll need them to drill holes in some hard drives to destroy sensitive information once you're over there. As you know, even when you delete a file from a computer, it is never completely deleted and can be recovered by any common computer geek. Anyway, everything will be explained to you by your counterparts once you're out there. Just think of this as a paid vacation, Andrew. Don't worry, this will be a walk in the park for you." His supervisor hangs up the phone after Andrew hesitantly agrees to go.

Andrew slowly sits back in his office chair and stares up at the ceiling while thoughts aggressively bounce around in his head. "I should be thanking my maker that they don't know about the files or the memory stick." He fidgets around in his chair arguing with himself and unable to get comfortable. "This timing couldn't be worse. Opportunity is finally knocking on my door while I'm tripping across the threshold of hell. I don't see an out here. I should just go and sort all this crap out when I get back." He continues mulling this over in his head thinking that he should feel lucky that opportunity is knocking on his door and not knocking it down, dragging him out and dumping his dead body in the river. While he nervously circles around his office trying to think of all the things he's going to need to do to prepare for his trip, his supervisor's secretary enters the room handing him his flight itinerary and hotel reservations. She tells him how lucky he is to be going to Seoul and that she always dreamed of going there herself. She also adds, "Guess who's been elected to pick up the morning coffee until you get back? That's right, you're looking at her. I won't be able to get even a single coffee order right. They'll have no mercy on me! Everyone is going to miss you, especially me. Please hurry back!" she exclaims.

After he finally settles down a bit, Andrew takes one more look at his mile high in-box and smiles to himself as he heads back home to pack. They told him he would be back in a week, so he counts out all his clothes. He stands in front of his filled suitcase and looks over his own body starting at his feet. "Let's see, shoes, socks, underwear, t-shirts, and dress shirts for seven days, check. That should do it." He also decides to bring his travel camera and his violin. He brings his violin with him on almost every trip since it is so small and easily fits in the plane's overhead compartment. Nights alone in hotels can be very lonely and having his music enables him to entertain himself. After a quick bite to eat and double checking that he has packed everything he needs for the trip including the tools he picked up, he checks the clock and re-checks the flight time. He catches himself before the words "It's go time" can slip out of his mouth. With violin case in hand, a backpack and his suitcase dragging behind him, he catches a glimpse of the lost keys on his desk. After a brief stare at this Pandora's box in the shape of a memory stick, on impulse he quickly drops everything and walks over to the desk, pulls the memory stick off the key ring and drops it into his pocket. He really doesn't want it on him but with so little time he can't figure out what else to do with it. So against his better judgement he will hide it in his violin case and not leave it behind.

After paying the taxi driver for the short ride, he grabs his bags and heads into the airport terminal. The terminal building has huge ceilings and fancy architectural supports crossing the center span giving you the feeling of being in a cathedral. It's a humbling feeling since you instantly feel somehow so small in comparison. You also get the impression that it's a great big world out there and these are the gates to that world. It's an impressive design as it should be. But big buildings can hold lots of people and today the terminal is packed. There are long lines everywhere and Andrew needs to find the right line to stand in. "Why doesn't this place make more sense?" he moans. He thinks to himself that they should have spent more time and money on organizing the many airlines rather than making the building look so impressive. After what seems like a quarter mile walk, he finally finds his airline and successfully figures out which line to stand in for the economy tickets. He can already imagine the two large men he will be sitting between for the next twenty hours on the flight. "At least the alcohol is free," he whispers under his breath.

After checking in and dropping off his bag, he heads toward the security checkpoint with several hundred people already standing in line in front of him. All he can do is people-watch as he shuffles along in a line that's reminiscent of a Disney attraction. Once he makes it to the front of the line, the pressure is now on. Take off your jacket, empty your pockets, pull your computer out of your backpack and place it in a separate bin, remove your belt, your shoes and do all this in 30 seconds because everyone behind you thinks you're taking too long. If they could press a hot cattle prod to your butt to get you to move faster, they would. Once you are half naked and standing on the yellow footprints on the hard rubber floor mat, you are then instructed to step into the scanner, spread your legs and put your hands above your head. Ironically, this is the same thing that happens when you're being arrested and handcuffed. "It sort of feels like you're guilty of something just standing here," Andrew thinks to himself. "If they only knew what's on that memory stick in my fiddle case that's probably showing up on the luggage x-ray screen right about now, I don't think I'd be getting on a plane anytime soon."

Finally Andrew makes his way to the terminal gate area and finds a seat. Looking around at the passengers waiting to board the plane, he notices how obvious it is that this is an Asian flight. The majority of the people have jet black straight hair, have full rounded faces, smooth skin and he can't understand anything they say as they speak with one another. The gate agent is making announcements about the boarding time and seating sequence arrangements beginning with first class, business class, women, children and the handicapped next, followed in the end by the cheap seats. This long and all too loud announcement is immediately repeated in its entirety in Korean. While waiting to board, there is nothing left to do but people-watch. Andrew knows about the racially insensitive stereotype that "Asians all look the same," but it appears to him that this is anything but true. Studying the people's faces around him clearly reveals that no one really looks alike and in fact everyone's facial features and overall look are as different as snowflakes. If there is anything at all about these people that is common, it is the peaceful look in their eyes. Not a single person appears to be stressed. This is very rare. Everyone, including Andrew is stressed just being in an airport. The days of travel being romantic and exciting with "champagne wishes and caviar dreams" is now a thing of the distant past.

People begin boarding and Andrew stands in line with the others being herded onto the plane. Of course he does not have a window seat or an aisle seat so he will be in constant competition for the use of the armrests for the next eighteen hours. "I should just draw a line down the center of each arm rest and tell these guys 'This half is yours and this half is mine. I paid full price for it!'" It's no use. They wouldn't understand him anyway.

The flight is brutally long. It would take a Buddhist monk in a deep meditative state to have the ability to sit still for such a long trip.   Actually everything about Andrew's life right now is unsettling. Attempting to sleep, read or find anything to ease his mind is fruitless. He settles on watching the flight progress on the seatback screen that shows a tiny plane following a curved path to his destination. It's on par with watching paint dry.

Andrew's flight is not direct so the longest segment of the flight takes place from Detroit to Seoul. This part of the flight is excruciatingly long and for sixteen hours he will have to endure episodes of crying children, short periods of his seat back being kicked by a young child and the complete inability to sleep sitting upright. When the pilot finally announces that the initial descent has begun, Andrew lets out a sigh of relief that can be heard by passengers all around him.

3. THE EAGLE HAS LANDED

Andrew has been awake for almost thirty hours when his plane finally touches down at Incheon Airport in Seoul. Being so far away from home is somehow a relief for him since there is only trouble waiting for him back there. Surprisingly he finds it a little easier to breath. It's like a heavy weight has been lifted from his chest. Once he makes it through customs and security, he finds the baggage claim turnstile and waits for his luggage to arrive. Andrew now has to change some American money to Korean currency and figure out how to get to the hotel. There is a currency exchange facility on his way out of the security checkpoint, so he stops to make an exchange to have local cash on hand. "I'd like to change two hundred and fifty American dollars to Korean won please," he asks the attendant. She replies in broken English that for an extra twenty-two dollars and fifty cents, she can give him an even two hundred and fifty thousand won. He agrees and after paying the balance, she proceeds to count out stacks of one thousand, five thousand, ten thousand and fifty thousand won bills. In the end, she stuffs a stack of bills an inch and a half thick into an envelope and hands it to him with his exchange receipt. Andrew was unaware of the exchange rate and picks up this thick envelope of money trying to decide what to do with it. It will never fit in his wallet and folding it in half only makes a three inch wad so in the end he sticks the entire envelope deep down in his front pocket so he won't lose it. He humorously thinks to himself that if this was two hundred and fifty thousand American dollars, both his car and apartment would be immediately upgraded.

The cheapest and most common transportation in Seoul is the bus services. He shows the bus station clerk at the ticket booth his hotel reservation and she pulls out a bus ticket and asks for ten thousand won. At first this amount seems outlandish until Andrew does the math in his head and realizes that the fee is about ten US dollars. With ticket in hand and bags in tow, he heads for the correct stop number and waits. The bus ride from the airport will take about an hour to reach his hotel area. The bus finally arrives and after settling into a seat he observes that the bus seems new and the seats are plush so the ride is smooth and comfortable. As burned out as Andrew is right now, he watches the scenery out the window with the intense interest of a child. The trip takes him by seemingly endless greenhouses among the open fields and also many miles of valuable ginseng crops that Korea is so famous for. Blue tarps hang like a sea of flags shading the young growing ginseng plants below. Dusk had shed enough light in the beginning of the bus ride so many things could be seen, but darkness has fallen quickly. This has ushered out the city lights which paint a warm glow across the night skyline. From the comfort of his seat, he can see the amazing lighting displays on the countless bridges that cross a land of endless rivers. Each bridge is different and is also lit differently. Just riding in this bus along the rivers and light show displays is fascinating enough to keep you awake no matter how tired you are. Andrew is convinced that the word Seoul must either mean river or bridge in Korean.

Finally, the bus pulls off the highway and slows down making its way into the city center. The city itself is lit up like Times Square in New York. Every business has neon signs and lights spelling out their names or some type of advertisement in Korean. Even though the signs are incomprehensible to him, the flashing and dancing lights are so alluring that Andrew can't wait to get off the bus and start exploring. The hotel is at the last stop. As the bus pulls away leaving Andrew standing right in the middle of a city pulsing with life, his sleep deprivation forces him to find the hotel, check in and then pass out in that order. Exploring the city will have to wait. He's now virtually brain dead and reading his map and identifying street signs at night is a challenge, but luck is on his side as he looks up, scans the buildings and finds the sign identifying the River View Hotel in bright lights. He drags his luggage and himself down the several streets leading to the hotel lobby entrance. The hotel is very impressive-looking and has a display in front of various countries' flags, reminiscent of the United Nations building. The hotel entry area is almost as grand as the airport terminals with towering marble columns and chandeliers. Walking up to the desk for check-in, he finds a Korean man and woman neatly dressed in suits bowing gently and welcoming him. During his check in, they take a copy of his credit card for incidentals but they explain that his company has set up direct billing with the hotel so all of his expenses during his stay will be covered and no charges will go on his own credit card. "Wow!" he says. "I'll have to bring back our company secretary something very special. Life is good!" They just smile at him and bow again. He is handed a room key and a stack of breakfast coupons almost as thick as his Korean currency envelope. "I'm sorry but I will be checking out in seven days. I don't think I will need all these breakfast coupons," he exclaims. The woman looks up from her computer screen and glances at her male associate who explains to Andrew that he should just take them anyway in case he loses or misplaces some. He walks away thinking that he can perhaps find some homeless people after his stay and give them free breakfasts for what looks like a month.

After exiting the elevator dragging his increasingly heavy bags behind him, he unlocks his hotel room door and dumps all his bags in a pile but carefully places his violin on the desktop. He removes his clothes, sets an alarm for his early morning meeting with the field team and shuts off the lights. He opens the curtains fully to reveal the night city skyline. Laying down in his bed, he manages to look out just long enough to catch a final view of the tall buildings and amazing night lights before his eyelids drop like a stone.

4. HURRY UP AND WAIT

Morning comes too quickly and the fourteen hour time difference between Washington and Korea will take some getting used to. Even though he got some sleep, Andrew is still mildly delirious and things don't seem as real to him as they normally do. He is caught between a dreamlike state and normal full awareness. He unpacks his bags and puts his toiletries in the bathroom. As he steps into the shower, he notices how low the shower head hangs. He thinks to himself that the Korean people are either smaller in general and the shower head height suits them just fine or this is the hotel's way of saving space. After a quick shower, Andrew gets dressed and heads down to the lobby. The elevator has a rear glass panel that reveals a stunning city view as it descends to the lobby.

Walking through the lobby he says good morning to the reception staff and makes his way to the breakfast buffet. After giving the hostess in the restaurant a single breakfast coupon, she seats him and walks away. He sits for a while and notices that everyone is just helping themselves to the large buffet spread and no one either asks for or is given menus. "I guess I'll just help myself then," he says out loud but softly enough so only he can hear it. The buffet is very large and is spread out along three long tables. Most of what is seen under the silver domes is unrecognizable. Andrew is very conservative when it comes to food so he attempts to fill his plate with only things he recognizes. Out of about sixty dish choices, he picks a scoop full of runny eggs that he first thought was some sort of egg drop soup. He then finds some rice with mixed vegetables that resembles fried rice that never touched a frying pan. The remainder of his plate is topped off with fruit.

Andrew samples a food offering called kimchi. He will soon learn that it is a very spicy oriental-style cabbage that is prepared in small tight rolls, tightly packed in large ceramic jars with lids and then buried underground for one month where one would naturally believe that it would slowly rot. But that is not exactly the case. The cabbage ferments and does not spoil. In fact it is a very traditional Korean dish and is very healthy for you. It's well known that every Korean family has their own recipe for kimchi. Once Andrew discovers the kimchi, he takes a large side dish of it. "It's like a cross between egg rolls and buffalo wings," he thinks to himself. Breakfast does not take long at all and afterwards he heads out to the lobby to wait for his contacts to meet him.

The lobby is still as impressive as it was when he walked in last night. Everything is clean and has a rich feel. As he sits down on a soft leather easy chair with a high back and plush armrests in full view of the revolving hotel door, he checks the time and finds he has a few minutes to rest his eyes. It's now eight o'clock and his team should be coming through the lobby doors any minute now. In the meantime, he begins to watch the hotel guests and staff wander about speaking Korean amongst themselves. He studies their facial expressions and the inflections in their voices as they speak. He's reminded of the many times he has watched movies on a plane with no audio. Either forgetting to bring his own headphones or the earbuds he had did not fit the special two-pronged connectors on the plane, he was forced to watch the equivalent of silent movies. Andrew had watched movies without audio often enough and he was always surprised how enjoyable they still were. Without hearing a word, he could focus on the actor's expressions, watch scenes play out and still easily follow the plot of the film. There were actual times on planes or even at home that he would watch movies without audio on purpose just to get a different perspective on things. He had come to the conclusion that it was not what people said but how they said it that mattered. A person's facial expressions, eye language or gaze and degree of relaxed composure or intensity as they spoke delivered as much information if not more than the words that came out of their mouth. It was the visual equivalent of speech inflection and today he was using these elements to study people speaking Korean in the hotel lobby. Even though the volume was not turned down and in fact the Koreans seemed to speak louder than typical English speakers, Andrew's study of their facial movements and features still gave him some sense of the nature of the conversation. A mother first yelling at a child running away across the lobby and then lecturing him upon his return as she zips up his jacket and fixes his hair delivers a conversation that almost anyone could understand in a non-verbal sense.

Andrew has been completely absorbed by this elevated form of people watching when he catches himself and looks at his watch. It's now well after 8 a.m. and there is no sign of his contacts. His agency had told him that they sent his picture to the team so no mistakes would be made in recognizing him. "They must be running late or in traffic," Andrew concludes. "I'll just have to wait." He continues people watching with the fascination of a child. New people check into the hotel and others are checking out, dragging their bags behind them. His contacts are now over two hours late and Andrew is becoming worried. He goes to the front desk and asks if any messages have been left for him. They bow politely to him and inform him that he has no messages.

Returning to his easy chair, he picks up one of the many magazines from a rack and sits back down to go through it and help pass the time. He strategically holds the magazine at such an angle that his face can clearly be seen by anyone entering the building. As he flips through the magazine that is almost an inch thick, he immediately realizes that the text is printed in Korean. There is not even a single word of English in the magazine, even in the advertising. But there are pictures: American faces and some presumably famous Korean faces, sometimes separate and sometimes together. It brings him back to his early childhood before he could read when all he could do was look at the pictures and imagine the story or make up his own. As he studies the appearance of the Korean models in the magazines and occasionally glances up at the people roaming and scurrying about in the lobby, they are somehow different. After some time, it occurs to Andrew that the Korean models chosen by the advertisers in the magazine look a little more American or at least European than Asian. At a minimum, the magazine models are a mix with parents of differing nationalities or they just simply have that unique look where on the one hand you can clearly recognize that they are Korean but at the same time would be attractive to an American and international audience. He wonders if this selection of cross-nationality-looking models is done intentionally with the sole purpose of selling products to a wider global audience. In advertising, very little is left to chance.

By the time Andrew has gone through his third magazine without recognizing a single word, he begins to feel that no one is coming for him. He reasons with himself that his company would not pay to send him all the way to Seoul for nothing, but still his rendezvous time has come and has long gone by without anyone approaching him or even giving him a second look. It is now lunch time and he figures that the best thing to do is to go to his room and order lunch instead of leaving the building. He leaves word at the desk that if anybody inquires about him, they are to ring his room and he will come down immediately. Lunch arrives and strangely resembles leftover breakfast buffet foods. "What I wouldn't do for a cheeseburger right now!" he exclaims. After lunch, he returns to the lobby, picks up yet another glamour magazine and drops himself down in his easy chair whose seat cushion still seems to be warm from his long morning. He switches back and forth between studying the faces of advertising models in the magazine and the continuous flow of people walking the grand hallway of the hotel. By sunset, he is convinced that either the date established for the meeting was wrong or his counterparts got the wrong hotel information. In either case, there is nothing he can do but wait.

He gives up his lobby easy chair and decides to get some dinner and then go out for a walk. The hotel has several different restaurants so he picks one that will have some western food options instead of strictly traditional Korean foods. The restaurant is very nice and the walls are lined with wine racks, books and art. Of course the books are not written in English but Andrew has come to expect that. The restaurant's idea of western food somehow still involves rice and unrecognizable vegetables but the food tastes good and is filling. The waitress that caters to him clearly does not speak English, but she is very kind and treats Andrew like royalty. He watches her as she moves from table to table taking care of everyone's needs and notices that she almost never stops moving, like a perpetual machine. She never sits down. At any given moment, she is either bringing food to a table or bringing empty plates away. In between tasks she stands like a statue with the eyes of a hawk scanning the room waiting for even the briefest of eye contact from a customer to set her in motion again. Andrew has eaten in restaurants back home for a good part of his life and has never seen such attentive service. It is very impressive.

He is still thinking about her sincere smile, flawless skin and neat appearance when he puts the meal on his room bill, tips her and thanks her as he leaves the restaurant. He heads back to the hotel desk asking for messages and learns he has none. "That's it. Enough for one day," he says under his breath. After returning to his room, he grabs his camera and coat and decides it's time to explore Seoul. It's not cold enough to snow but still it is quite cool outside: just right for a long walk. In the city center of Seoul, the night lights and city scape are breathtaking. Red tail lights line the busy streets as cars make their way around the city. You can smell the aroma of local coffee shops and small restaurants cooking food. Patrons can be seen through the windows conversing and dipping their chopsticks into small bowls and dishes. There are so many brightly lit business signs seemingly in every window, on every floor of every building that it's questionable if street lights are really necessary at all. As Andrew walks along the streets his jacket reflects the different neon sign colors as if he were walking through a water color painting with pigment colors rubbing off on him. He feels like he has taken on the powers of a chameleon with his face lighting up to match the intense reds, blues and greens of one lighted business sign after another.

The characters that make up the Korean language fascinate him. Andrew has traveled to other countries and some Spanish or Italian words are close enough to English to enable a fair guess at what they mean, but Korean is much different. In a quick Google search before his trip, he found that the Korean text characters are very similar to Chinese characters. Each character set represents a word or part of a word that can be translated into alphabetical letters that has some measure of equivalent sound in English but that's where the similarities abruptly end. So the characters or text symbols are like a shorthand version of an alphabetical word or phrase such as "gamsahabnida." The words are long so the shorthand symbols make perfect sense. The only thing that makes no sense to Andrew are the resulting words. There is no way a person can guess the English equivalent of "gamsahabnida." It means "thank you" but Andrew does not know even this much. He instead just studies the symbols, how they are arranged and how cool they look. Even though they have a meaning that he is unable to decode, they are still interesting to look at and study - almost like watching his "silent movies" on the plane.

After getting enough fresh cold air in his lungs and walking leisurely for hours, Andrew decides to head back to the hotel and call it a night. The hotel clerk tells him in broken English, "No message" even before he is in front of the desk. Somehow, he had been ok with the idea that his meeting time or location had been mixed up, but now he is becoming deeply concerned. "Maybe tomorrow," he tells the clerk and wishes him a good night. He makes it back to his room, puts his camera away and prepares for bed. He turns on the television in his room and is unable to find a channel broadcasting anything in English so he falls asleep to a Korean made-for-TV movie with the volume turned down.

5. SAME STUFF – DIFFERENT DAY

The morning sun as seen through the window from the upper floor of the hotel is uniquely beautiful. The sun itself is a deep red color and the light emanating from it is weak enough for you to stare directly into it without hurting your eyes. Andrew looks at the Korean flag in front of the hotel after staring at the sun making its way above the distant mountains. He concludes that the inspiration for the yin yang sun symbol illustrated in the center of the flag must be due to this stunning sunrise. Half of the yin yang sun is as red as the sun is right now and the other half is sky blue, the same color of the morning sky. He wonders why he did not notice the beautiful sunrise yesterday. After getting himself showered he heads downstairs with another coupon for breakfast. Passing the front desk clerks and gently bowing has now become a tradition for him even though this is only day three. Breakfast is no surprise, even though Andrew thought the buffet would change day to day. After checking every silver heated chafing dish, he finds that every food item in the buffet is the same as it was yesterday. "Maybe they change the menu every week," he thinks to himself. "At least I hope so. If not, I'm going to slowly starve." He makes the same breakfast selections as he did yesterday and sits down to eat. He realizes that in all of his selections there is no meat - not even in the rice. Circumstances being what they are, he is eating vegetarian breakfasts. It's only then that he misses the smell and flavor of bacon. In his mind he can just see it sizzling in the pan and turning golden brown as he passively picks up a clump of rice with his chopsticks. "Oh well, I'll be back home in a few days and that will be one of the first things I cook," he insists.

After breakfast, he goes right for the magazine rack and is seated in the lobby before 8 a.m. But again, to his dismay, eight o'clock comes and goes without contact. He remains in the lobby all morning and with each passing minute, he can feel his vegetarian breakfast churning and tumbling inside his stomach. Something is very wrong. No one has shown up and now Andrew has the sickening feeling that no one is actually going to show up. He starts examining his options at this point since there really was no Plan B, so to speak. He is not allowed to contact his contracting agency since his mission is covert. There is also no one he can call back in the US to discuss his situation. He begins to get the sinking feeling that he is going to be stuck there if no one shows up or at least until his return flight at the end of the week. After lunch, he makes a decision to stay the course and try to enjoy the rest of his stay. Things are really out of his hands now so he might as well make the best of it. He is, after all, in a very big and beautiful city surrounded by culture and sights just waiting to be explored.

His own Plan B for the remainder of his stay will be to get breakfast in early each day and then wait a few hours in the lobby in case someone does show up. After that, he will be off on the less beaten paths outside with his camera. His own supervisor did tell him that this was going to be like a paid vacation, he recalls. "Maybe these people just didn't need me after all," Andrew says to console himself. "Paid vacation? I'll take it!"

Today is another sunny day with almost no wind but still cool. He bundles up for an afternoon on the town. During his walk, he finds that in general the main streets are lined with very expensive and very exclusive stores such as Gucci and Bvlgari. Behind large glass windows are high-end car dealerships such as Lamborghini, Ferrari and Jaguar. The displays go on as far as the eye can see. There are people with a lot of money here, he concludes. In fact a person standing on one of the main roads of downtown Seoul could easily be mistaken by thinking he was right in the middle of New York City. However, just one street parallel but set back off the main road is an endless array of more affordable food stores, clothing shops and restaurants. The further off the main roads Andrew wanders, the more traditional the home construction becomes and the feel of being in a foreign land becomes increasingly prominent.

There are however some constants about this distant city; both the food (for the most part) and the language are unrecognizable. Anyone Andrew stops in the street or in the market to ask for directions or the most basic questions are completely unable to understand him. They just smile politely and shrug their shoulders and say "joesonghabnida" (sorry). "That is so not helpful," Andrew says to himself. He bows to show them respect and moves on. There are a few specific foods that he can recognize but has never eaten nor would even consider. One is octopus. This is on the menu of virtually every restaurant he passes and there is even one location that serves it live and freshly chopped up. Andrew thinks to himself "I would rather starve than eat something still moving on my plate, even if it tastes like chicken." There's also a fast food vendor that serves octopus legs batter fried with a side of French fries. "Now I know I'm not in Kansas anymore," he tells himself jokingly.

Another thing he notices in the front display of certain restaurants is a fish tank filled with something that looks like it has one half of an oyster shell and the unprotected exposed side is a cross between a slug and a sucker fish. They are crawling around the surface of the glass tank and are beginning to gross him out. Once he finds a single empty shell in a barrel he passes, he recognizes the vivid reflective colors of the shell's interior surface. It is abalone. Andrew concludes that abalone must be a delicacy since it is a prominent restaurant food item. However, he decides to pass on trying it himself. He finds it surprising how many common Korean foods there are out here that would never be found on a menu back in the US. What he is unable to find is burger joints, roast beef, fried chicken or any of the other foods he is craving. He can't even find a hotdog!

6. A CHANGING WIND

Two hundred and fifty thousand won seems like a lot of money but relative to the dollar and the cost of products, it is not. So Andrew buys a few small souvenirs and decides to make his way back to the hotel to eat. After lunch he heads back up to his room. He sees a cleaning lady working on one of the rooms close to his. As he gets closer to his hotel door while checking all his pockets for the key, the cleaning woman comes out of the other room, looks at him and smiles. Andrew says hello and recognizes the woman from the hotel restaurant last night. She was his waitress. He wonders if she ever stops working. She is like a perpetual machine. He bows his head to her gently and says, "Good day." Knowing that she does not understand, he feels compelled to say it anyway as a show of respect. He continues thinking about her as he enters his room closing the door behind him. After putting his things away, he decides to play his violin before taking a short nap. He pulls out some sheet music and plays a beautiful piece that sounds like a cross between classical material and a soft lullaby. Although he tries to play the violin softly, it is still loud enough for the cleaning lady to enjoy. She pauses for a few moments to listen each time she comes out of the rooms she is cleaning to get supplies from her cart. After about an hour of playing music, Andrew puts his instrument down and lays back on the neatly folded bed linen to rest his eyes. Although it seems like he has only slept an hour or two, when he gets up he finds that the sun has set and evening has set in. "I must have really needed that sleep," he remarks. He tosses open the curtains to reveal the fully lit evening skyline which is just about as beautiful as the sunrise. In awe, he whispers "Wow!"

Later in the evening while heading down to the hotel restaurant, he stops by the front desk to find no messages as usual. He is cordially seated in what is now his usual spot in the restaurant and is handed a menu. He spots the same waitress who doubles as the cleaning lady by day and even before they make eye contact, she is already on the move and heading in his direction. She smiles for him again and looks towards the menu prompting Andrew to point to his food selection. Like throwing a dart at a dartboard blindfolded, he randomly puts his finger on a menu item having no idea what it actually is. He also stands up and walks her over to a bottle of red wine on the rack asking for a glass with his meal. She bows gracefully and smiles once again as she walks away to place his order. He notices that she does not wear a lot of makeup beyond a touch of lipstick. Her skin is amazingly smooth and her face is very attractive. She has a peaceful look about her even though most of her waking hours are spent working. She walks away and Andrew soon realizes that he did well with his choice of wine and the meal since they were both very good. When the waitress returns after a short time to see if there is anything else needed, Andrew asks if she can tell him her name. She is not really understanding his question so he points to himself as if acting out a game of charades and says slowly, "My name is Andrew Trainor." Then he points to her and asks even more slowly, "What is your name?" "Ji-woo Cho," she replies as she points to herself. "Thank you Ji-woo. The food and service here are excellent!" Andrew replies. After putting the bill on his room tab, tipping Ji-woo and bowing to honor the restaurant staff for the evening, he heads out to the lobby to decide what to do next.

He decides to relax at a bar over a few drinks since the wine at diner has put him in a good mood. The hotel has a selection of various restaurants and bars so he heads to a small bar on the top floor of the hotel that he learns about from the front desk staff. The panoramic view of the city is stunning. "Why didn't I find this place before?" he asks himself. He sits at the bar and orders a beer. The bar is quiet and empty aside from the female bartender and a few couples sitting at tables enjoying the city view. As Andrew lifts his glass of draft beer and tilts his head back for his first long sip, he notices a large TV screen on the wall above the bar. He looks at it and wonders why there is no soccer or golf games being viewed. The bartender has been watching the local news. She probably has no interest in sports anyway. As Andrew enjoys his ice cold beer, he watches the news and notices that there are English subtitles scrolling along the bottom of the screen. Finally after three days, he can at least understand something in his native tongue.

After what appeared to be several headline world news topics, an image appears on the screen that the reporters indicate involves breaking news. Andrew quickly drops his beer down on the bar and is in utter shock as he stares at his own picture on the TV screen. The TV reporter states that the American pictured here has been accused of being a foreign spy against the South Korean government and is being sought after for questioning. The citizens of Seoul are being asked to report any information about him directly to authorities and to be aware that he may be dangerous. For a solid minute, Andrew is unable to breath, move or even think. "Holy Shit!!" he exclaims uncontrollably. He quickly fumbles through his wallet, slaps twenty thousand won down on the bar for his beer and races out into the hallway toward the elevators. He is in absolute shock. He also feels he is in imminent danger and his survival instincts are telling him to run - anywhere!

He pushes the elevator button, repeatedly blurting out, "Come on! Come on!" He jumps through the first elevator doors that open and presses his floor number while thoughts thrash through his brain in a desperate attempt to understand what has just happened. He decides to get to his room, quickly pack and take the staircase down to get outside and grab a cab to the airport. Once he exits the elevator, he tries to calm himself down and stop running. He reaches his room, grabs his key and opens his door. Inside his room are several Korean government authorities, some local police officers and the hotel manager waiting for him. The hair on Andrew's neck is standing out as pulses of electric shock run up and down the length of his spine. The group rush him and he is immediately handcuffed. He is brought down to a conference room where he is interrogated - all the while maintaining his innocence and constantly repeating "You have the wrong guy!" Later, after leading him down to a large conference table that was clearly set up ahead of time with a neatly dressed tablecloth, folded napkins and water glasses at each seating, the remaining people in the room also sit down and quietly stare at Andrew.

Suddenly, one of the government officers breaks the silence and begins to speak. He speaks English fairly well. He states, "My name is Yejun Kwon and I am an intelligence officer out of our Seoul office. Our Korean Intelligence Agency received a tip that you were in our country and had come here to steal nuclear power plant blueprints and collect facility images to support a planned terrorist attack aimed at destroying our power infrastructure and destabilizing our economy. Andrew's jaw drops and he strongly denies this claim. Although he cannot reveal the true nature of his visit, he tells them that he is just vacationing. Yejun continues, "Is this your camera, computer and cell phone that we brought down with us from your room?" Andrew examines the devices and agrees that they belong to him. The officials had brought all of Andrew's electronic devices with them to the interrogation room. Yejun pulls the memory stick out of Andrews's camera, places it inside Andrews's computer and asks him to turn it on and allow it to boot up. He then takes the computer back and opens the contents of the memory stick. All the men get up from their seats and closely examine the monitor as Yejun studies the files opening them one by one. He then opens a folder and finds a number of pictures of the Shin Hanul Nuclear Power Plant along with pictures taken of blueprint drawings showing the plant's internal structures and layout. All the men looking at the computer screen gasp and begin speaking in Korean to each other quite loudly. Yejun quickly spins the laptop around so Andrew can see the evidence for himself while commenting, "Vacationing?" Andrew immediately fires back, "That is not my picture and I have no idea how it got on my camera! You've got to believe me. I had nothing to do with that and in fact I never left Seoul at all since I got here. How could I have taken those pictures?" "That's what we would like to know and what we plan on finding out. Clearly this is your camera and you are responsible for the contents of your own property. I'm afraid we have no choice but to place you under arrest while we try to sort this out. This is a very serious crime Mr. Trainor and we don't take threats like this lightly," states the officer. Andrew replies, "Please, please, I beg of you. Investigate this matter further and you will find I am innocent. Someone must have planted those files on my camera because they certainly did not get there on my account." "Mr. Trainor, we will without question investigate this matter, but until we have a chance to prove things one way or another, you will be placed under house arrest here at the hotel. Trust me when I tell you that we are giving you the benefit of the doubt and are showing great leniency by not placing you directly into our jail system. However, we will be monitoring your location every minute of the day. You will be allowed to go outside but you must remain within a ten block radius and must return to your room every evening. Any attempt to leave the ten block area of the hotel will result in your immediate transfer to a maximum security prison until your trial. Is this clear Mr. Trainer?"

Andrew agrees to the terms but adamantly reiterates his innocence. "This is a set-up Mr. Kwon. I will follow your rules to the letter but please keep me abreast of the results of your investigation. Am I allowed to go now?" "Yes, you are but we will be confiscating all of your electronic devices and I'm afraid you are going to have to give me your passport and credit cards until your innocence is proven." Andrew hands over his passport and credit cards but is allowed to keep his cash. He returns to his room.

He is still in shock and cannot believe what has just transpired. "What the hell just happened?" he shouts at himself. "Where did that shit on my camera come from?" He retraces his steps in his mind through every single detail of his day, the day before and the day before that. Someone got into his room and installed those files on his camera memory stick; that much is certain. But, who and why?

Andrew is left with no ability to communicate with the outside world and dejectedly concludes that no one is coming to help him. There will be no navy seal recovery team dropping down ropes from a helicopter and smashing though his hotel room window to grab him and whisk him off to safety. He has never felt so alone in his entire life. After laying back in his recliner staring at the ceiling for hours while maddening thoughts torture his crippled mind, his brain finally resets and he eventually passes out fully dressed and frozen in position.

CHARLES MICHAEL LANDRY

7. THE AFTER MATH

Morning brings a waking Andrew back to reality with a sore neck and a headache. The first moment that he regains partial consciousness is almost blissful since he has no idea where he is or what has happened. This only lasts a split second before he realizes he fell asleep in his clothes and the events of last night were not just a bad dream, they were painfully real. He stares into space at nothing in particular for almost fifteen minutes while he tries to digest the evening's events and his current predicament. He forces himself to get up and take a shower but everything he does now is in slow motion. It takes real effort to even hold his toothbrush and move it around his mouth. After he is cleaned up, he realizes that he really did all this for nothing. Since his face as been plastered all over TV and the entire country now sees him as a criminal in spite of his innocence, he is too embarrassed to leave his room and show his face in public.

He falls back onto the bed and thinks about routine things that he would be doing in Korea like eating breakfast, "reading" Korean magazines or going out for a walk and some fresh air but they are not options for him today. He cannot force himself to eat and even gives up on the idea of ordering room service. On a whim, he flips on the TV and after a few commercials, he sees the news report about his involvement in the alleged spy scandal and immediately shuts the TV off before his face is shown on the screen again. From this point on they might as well just take the TV out of his room because he has absolutely no intention of ever turning it on again. He puts the TV remote control in the nightstand drawer next to a religious book on Buddhism and slams the drawer shut. He pulls the shades, puts the "Do Not Disturb" sign on his hotel room's outer door handle, takes off his cloths and falls back into bed. For the remainder of the day, he isolates himself in his room and gets only brief periods of sleep after his racing mind temporarily exhausts him. Darkness eventually falls but this only intensifies Andrew's feeling of isolation.

The next morning, he gets up and goes through the same routine struggling to shower and shave with motions that are more mechanical than ever. It is like part of his mind has shut down and his body is on autopilot going through motions without his usual conscious involvement. Although he is mentally numb after hours of staring out the window at the cars and people milling about, he finally makes a decision to venture outside. His logic and some familiar brain function is starting to kick in and he realizes that just staying isolated in his room will eventually drive him to madness. He grabs his coat, wallet and room key and heads for the door. Getting off the elevator into the main lobby, he keeps his head down, walks past the front desk and makes his way outside. Painfully aware of his ten block roaming limit he begins his walk, reminding himself to count the streets as he goes. Many people he encounters avoid eye contact with him as soon as they recognize him from the news as the American terrorist. Andrew begins to notice this happening quite often and couples or groups do the same in unison while talking in Korean amongst themselves. "Jeug, seupai ibnida" (That is the spy!) are the most common words he hears from group to group as he makes his way down the street. Andrew is beginning to feel like he has three eyes or that his face is permanently disfigured like the title character from *The Elephant Man*. As difficult as this is to accept, his mind is so crippled that these observations begins to matter less and less to him as the afternoon passes. He will have to harden his heart if he is to survive.

Somehow Andrew feels a slight sense of relief just being out of the hotel and walking in the fresh air. The air itself is still cool but the sun feels warm on his face. Spring in Seoul is arriving and he can see the trees and flowers are beginning to bud. The city is bustling with activity as trucks make deliveries, people are moving in every direction and cars chaotically fly through the streets as if the speed limits, traffic lights and street signs do not apply to them. There are also many scooters buzzing about. Some of them have insulated boxes mounted on the back for delivery of food and packages. Desperate to stop his brain from being fixated on his problems, Andrew occasionally closes his eyes briefly as he walks past a coffee shop or restaurant so he can take in the full experience of the aromatic air. These alluring smells are perhaps the best form of advertisement. Especially with a bakery or patisserie, only the strongest willed individuals can keep themselves from walking in and picking out one of everything that looks good. This only serves to tease Andrew since walking into any shop, even to buy coffee, is out of the question for him now. Walking the city streets starts to involve all of his physical senses. This seems to be just what his mind needs to reset and clear his negative energy. He has a lot of clearing to do.

Andrew is not aware that he has forgotten to count the streets and eventually finds two police cars parked on the corner of what must be the tenth street; his outer limit. The officers are staring right at him. Not willing to "test the fence" for weaknesses, he turns himself right back around and takes a different street back toward the hotel. All of the walking and fresh air have given Andrew some of his appetite back. He finds many street vendors with carts setup cooking fresh fast foods that a person can grab and eat on the go. Unfortunately, the food is difficult to recognize and identify. It occurs to Andrew that most people have a basic need to know what a food is before they are willing to even taste it. As bad as hot dogs are for you, which is common knowledge in the United States, they are immediately recognized and still taste good therefore they are a big seller. He recalls visiting a restaurant in the state of Maine where they had hot dogs that had a red outer casing. It was just a hot dog but Andrew could not bring himself to even try it. The taste of the red hot dogs were probably the same as the normal colored hot dogs but our brains are programmed for familiarity. Maybe this is some protective lower brain function to prevent people from poisoning themselves.

During his walk, he comes across a vendor selling chunks of sweet potato skewered on a stick that have been baked and dipped in a sweet honey glaze. They smell delightful and look incredible. He is unable to resist and buys a stick. They are 1,000 won each and are worth every Korean penny. The vendor himself is an older man and has the most peaceful disposition Andrew has encountered in Seoul since he arrived. Somehow he either does not recognize Andrew from TV News or does not watch TV. Andrew pays the man, they bow to each other showing mutual respect and he takes his sweet potato stick to go while enjoying it on his walk back to the hotel. He has gone without food too long now and the vendor food makes him realize just how hungry he is. Returning to the hotel, he orders room service and eats what he can, but his appetite has once again diminished.

Over the next several days, Andrew continues to venture outside, but he is still continually being recognized and pointed out like a Hollywood celebrity except no one is happy to see him nor wants an autograph. The sounds of the city and the sounds of people's voices are beginning to get louder and louder with each passing day. Andrew is recognizing this but is choosing to ignore it. On one afternoon walk as he was halfway back to the hotel, he finds a small indoor restaurant serving noodle soups. He decides to take a chance, walks in and attempts to speak with the host to order a meal. The host does not speak English and Andrew suspects by his reaction that he recognizes him from the newscast. The man quite loudly asks Andrew to leave or something to that effect since he is pointing to the outside door and verbalizing a flurry of intimidating sounding words in Korean. Even with no knowledge of the Korean language Andrew gets the message and leaves the restaurant, continuing on his walk as he tries to let this upsetting episode roll off his shoulders.

Yet something has now changed in Andrew's perception of the Korean language after this encounter. It seems that people are now speaking even louder than before, much louder. Even people walking the streets casually speaking with each other are being perceived by Andrew as if someone has turned up the volume on a radio to maximum. Suddenly the city scenery and aromatic scent of budding flowers are completely dulled by the loud voices of people in the streets. Andrew attempts to analyze why this is happening since it does not look like people are actually shouting at each other. He realizes it is his own perception of the voices that has become super sensitized. As he walks back to the hotel he is hoping that this is just a temporary effect that will wear off soon, but it does not. Back in the hotel, once inside the grand entry, the combined voices of over twenty people and a cacophony of other sounds bouncing off tall marble walls hits Andrew like the sonic boom of a military jet breaking the sound barrier. He races for the elevator. As the elevator rises, he fumbles for the keys to his room. Silence welcomes him once inside his hotel room and he drops down on the bed. He lays motionless until the noise reverberating inside his head diminishes. Andrew is beginning to believe that he is losing his sanity. In the process of his self-analysis, he falls asleep.

8. SILENCE IS GOLDEN

Andrew wakes up to sunlight pouring through his room window warming and lighting up his face. He turns over onto his back in bed and as reality slowly sets in he again begins to feel his state of isolation with agonizing acuity. In his mind he visualizes the entire scope of the planet Earth as if he is hovering out in space. His image zooms in slowly to Asia, then South Korea, then to Seoul and then finally to the view of his body lying on his bed. There is nowhere for him to turn to for assistance and as he rolls himself into a tight fetal position, he now feels more alone than ever before.

The painful irony of being surrounded by twenty million people in this city while being denied basic human needs such as freedom and the ability to communicate for such a long period of time is beginning to take its toll. We are a social species and solitary confinement goes against our very nature. It is clearly a form of torture that may be tolerable in the beginning but builds in intensity over time to a point of being totally unbearable. Andrew sees what is happening to himself and feels he is helpless in resolving it. It dawns on him that people who talk to themselves in public are viewed by others as crazy, but just maybe they talk to themselves to keep from going insane.

Crazy or not, Andrew feels an even more basic and essential need right now and that is his survival. His life must go on and he must hold together some semblance of normalcy if he is to survive. He mumbles, "I could just hang myself from the shower head and put an end to all this misery. If only it was mounted a little higher off the floor." He quickly shakes his head to snap himself out of his self-destructive state of mind and to focus on the day ahead of him. "Hell, I'm innocent and there's got to be a way to prove it," he reminds himself. "Let's just try to take things one hour at a time."

He shuffles his way into the shower and then eventually makes his way down to the buffet for breakfast. Suddenly it occurs to him that something was very wrong with his getting such a big stack of breakfast coupons when he checked into the hotel on his first day in Seoul. It was as if someone knew before he even arrived that his stay was going to be extended. As disturbing as this point is, it gives Andrew a clue to ponder over. Heaven knows that he has plenty of pondering time. He comes to the conclusion while eating runny eggs that someone in the hotel had to have the foreknowledge that he was going to be set up. As he finishes breakfast he decides that he now had a new mission in life: to connect the dots and figure out who has set him up and why. This will take time and will not be easy since he does not speak Korean. He is going to have to fight this battle on his own, but at least now there may be some hope.

So much hope in fact that he decides to return to his normal routine of going out for his daily walks. However, the amplified foreign language is still a problem for him. He concludes that he should rest during the day, play his music and take his walks during the evening hours when the number of people on the streets and the noise in general is greatly diminished. This decision works very well for him as the darkness brings him anonymity, peace and clarity of mind. He will follow this new routine for the next few weeks only venturing out for short periods in daylight to see things like the new cherry blossoms and the exotic Korean flowers that spring is beginning to usher in.

The evening walks are all very nice in the beginning and he is able to hold things together for a while. But over time he once again begins to lose hope of finding more clues and proving his innocence. No one will speak with him and instead simply chose to avoid him. His relatively brief period of hope is beginning to slowly erode.

During a long walk one evening, Andrew finds himself drawn into a small electronics shop. He finds that they have many inexpensive appliances, but one item in particular that catches his attention is an audio tape player and recorder. It is older technology and he is surprised to find that they still exist, but they apparently are still making them somewhere in Asia. The sign says "two for one" and the price is twenty thousand won. He decides to buy two and some blank cassette tapes to go with them. He thinks he will use the device to begin recording a daily diary of his experiences. He figures that the second one will come in handy if the first one brakes which, based on the price, is a virtual certainty. Besides, it is free. He hopes that he will find some comfort in recording his voice and listening to it play back as it will be his only source of fluent English language.

On another one of his nightly walks, he ends his evening with a visit to the hotel karaoke bar. He orders a few beers and listens to the locals sing Beatles songs and other American classic hits in "Korenglish"; a source of great amusement for him. It isn't English but it is close and he loves the music. Inspired by the music and the alcohol, he returns to his room and plays the violin for a few hours before settling in for the night. Eventually, this becomes more and more of a nightly routine for him as he realizes that the alcohol and the alluringly distracting music will allow him forget his situation and find some comfort. One night, the bartender gives him a shot glass of a local traditional drink called soju. It is very strong, made from rice and is reminiscent of sake. It seems to be the Korean equivalent of a mind-eraser cocktail. Andrew becomes very fond of this local spirit and begins to enjoy it a little too much. After a few hours of soju-laden karaoke, he is carefree and can muster up a smile. Andrew knows enough to not go overboard with it and make a fool of himself, but still what he is trying to erase will always come back to him the following morning with a hangover companion.

One evening after drinking heavily, Andrew stumbles back to his room and even though he is in no condition to play at his usual level, he picks up his violin and opens the small compartment to get the rosin for his bow and there it is - the memory stick, forgotten all this time in his violin case. Even the police and intelligence officers did not find it - or perhaps did not even bother to look. An intense rage overcomes him at that point and he wishes that he had never been born. Putting his violin away and closing the case, he lays back on the bed and deliberates in his mind the options he has at his disposal to end his life. Hanging himself would not work in his room, he has no access to pills and he can't slice his wrists with a butter knife. He fights to stay awake to settle on a solid self-termination plan but he loses the battle and passes out for the evening.

After waking up with a hangover the following morning, and uttering the words "Now I really wish I were dead," something deep inside of Andrew's aching brain bubbles its way to his surface awareness and he knows with all his heart that he was not put on this planet only to have his life end this way - without purpose. There is a reason he is here, on this planet, at this time and it is not to come this far just to take his own life. Even if he does not know what life ultimately has in store for him, he knows that this present situation is not it; there has to be more. It is time now to pull himself together, leave the soju for others to enjoy and put his life back in order even if it is an impossible situation. He showers and goes down for breakfast like the good old days. He didn't appreciate until now that feeling so good could come about by just letting go and accepting the present totality of his life. After a late afternoon nap, he wakes up feeling better still and that normalcy has returned to his life; even if being under house arrest is to be a part of it.

Hunger has set in so he decides to return to Ji-woo's restaurant for a good meal. Just the act of temporarily putting his situation aside gives him enough space in his busy mind to enjoy her company. After sitting down at his usual table, she comes over to him with his menu. Bending over to show him the food selections, she uses her finger and points to a meal that she thinks he would enjoy. She says, "Very good!" Andrew agrees to her meal selection and is happy to see her English vocabulary is expanding. She again smiles and gently bows as she walks away. This smile is different somehow. It speaks plainly to Andrew saying "I like you." At least that is the interpretation Andrew wants to hear. He also notices that while in her presence, she is all he can think about. Like the mind-eraser cocktail, her image makes all of his problems dissolve into the ether. In the words of the Beatles song from the karaoke bar, "Got to Get You into My Life," Andrew begins to develop a new mission in life; to spend more time with Ji-woo. The meal she brings out is traditional Korean food but is remarkably delicious. When he finishes his meal, Andrew thanks Ji-woo repeatedly, pays the bill and finds himself staring at her. Smiling to himself, he is wishing at this moment with all his might that he had the ability to speak even a dozen Korean words. She then surprises him once again saying, "Good evening." He responds, "And a very good evening to you also." They bow to each other and part ways. Her image will accompany him on his evening walk and for the rest of his night.

9. A VOICE IN THE NIGHT

Andrew has wandered through every street within his ten block radius by now. Some of the streets are more to his liking than others, but tonight with Ji-woo still smiling in his mind, he finds himself walking on air in no particular direction. The architecture of the buildings in this area of Seoul is beyond beautiful. They are unique and are visually stunning especially with the strategic use of the lighting incorporated in the design. Everything in the city seems brighter tonight. Even the taxis that far outnumber the passenger cars on the roads are lit up with red "for hire" neon signs in their windows that seem to twinkle as they fly by. The trees that line the roads have been pruned back to an almost extreme extent but Andrew notices how strangely beautiful these bare trees are against the backlit buildings. What is so unusual is that there are so many of these trees and they are all impeccably pruned. "It must take an army of arborists to handle the sheer volume of pruning required for every tree in this city alone," Andrew thinks to himself. "Why do they even bother?"

As he passes a tall building that is either under construction or is being renovated, his mind wandering a million miles away, something catches Andrew's attention. Large sheets of plastic hiding construction work behind them are being gently moved about by the wind. Up until now as he has roamed the city streets, he has been completely unaware of any breeze. Suddenly a voice calls out from behind the plastic, "Hello." Andrew's head snaps back with such velocity that he falls just short of giving himself whiplash. Totally startled and not knowing if he actually heard a real voice or if his mind is playing tricks on him, he responds, "Is someone there?" "You are the spy, aren't you?" responds the mysterious voice. "I am not a spy!" Andrew shouts back and continues, "That is an outright lie. Where are you?" "Are you dangerous? Will you hurt me?" replies the voice that Andrew is now convinced is that of a child. "No, certainly not. I have never hurt anyone," Andrew responds defensively. "Well then I am just behind the plastic sheets in the work zone. You may come in," replies the voice.

Andrew draws back one of the hanging plastic sheets in the general direction the voice came from and finds a small boy sitting on a tool chest. The boy has short, dark hair, bright, piercing eyes and looks to be about twelve to fifteen years old. "I've been watching you. You walk these streets often. You are the criminal I saw on TV. Why do you want to come here and hurt us?" the boy asks. "That is not true," Andrew replies. "Everything you heard on TV is a lie. I have been set up. I don't know who did this to me or why, but there is not much I can do about it. I have been framed and if there is a criminal here, it is someone from your own country and not me. I just can't prove it right now," replies Andrew. Suddenly Andrew realizes that he is having an English conversation for the first time in over a month and he asks the boy, "What's your name?" "Ki Young. What is your name?" replies the boy. "My name is Andrew. Isn't it a bit late for you to be out?" inquires Andrew. "My father works late and my mother is away visiting," replies Ki Young and continues, "Right now I am at home playing video games - except I'm not. I am here with you. How do I know I can trust you?" "Listen." Andrew pleads with the boy. "I would never hurt you. I am a good person." Andrew and the boy stare at each other, gauging each other's trust. "If you can trust me and help me translate some things, I may be able to prove my innocence. No one will speak with me so as of this moment you are my only hope. Please believe me." "OK Mr. Andrew, I have to go now but I will see you again. Maybe you can tell me about America. Also, do not look for me or mention my name. I will find you. We will speak again soon," Ki Young responds. He jumps down off the tool chest and walks toward the rear of the building into the darkness. Andrew is stunned but there is a glimmer in his eyes as he heads back out into the street and starts making his way back to the hotel. For the first time in a very long time Andrew feels his own heart beating again. With solemn gratitude he feels the gentle night breeze against his cheeks. There may finally be hope.

On his way back into the hotel he pauses briefly in front of the front desk and gently bows to the staff. The staff look at one another in wonder and hesitantly bow in return. "This is a new day," Andrew says softly under his breath as he walks to the elevator. He presses his floor button and waits for his scenic night view lift to his hotel room. Once inside his room, he picks up the tape recorder and dictates another entry into his audio diary that he started some time ago. He also wants to record Ki Young and Ji-woo's names and correct pronunciation so he does not forget them. A lot happened today so his diary entry is lengthy. He plays the recording back a few times to enjoy listening to his dictation entry in English.

Andrew sleeps well through the night. Feeling rested the next morning he washes up and heads down for his usual breakfast. It appears they have changed the breakfast menu a bit. Now the fried rice is mixed with kimchi for breakfast. "Perfect," he says sarcastically as he grabs a big scoop of it and hopes for the best. The rest of the breakfast items appear to be unchanged. Feeling good this morning, he decides to change up his routine and gets orange juice instead of his usual pineapple juice. "What the hell, just go wild," he thinks to himself.

After breakfast he heads out to the streets. He notices that people are not looking at his American face and identifying him as "the criminal" so much anymore and the more time goes on, people in general are beginning to forget all about him and the alleged incident. There are brief interludes when even he forgets. A person can get used to just about anything and now even Andrew's former life back home is becoming a faded memory. During his walk this morning he realizes that he is beginning to see things that he never noticed before. Even though brightly colored flowers are lining the city streets in a beautiful display, Andrew notices that some of the trees have not yet begun to fully develop leaves. Somewhere close to the top of these trees there is a one foot diameter birds nest in the shape of a perfect sphere. He wonders what kind of bird makes these nests since they are so unusual in their roundness. It makes the upper part of the trees look like the tail of a French poodle. Like many other things in life, once you see something that grabs your attention, you begin to see it everywhere. Andrew now sees that these bird nests are in about every fourth tree in the area. They are not on the pruned trees, however. He ponders over these things as he enjoys the fresh air and lingers a little longer than usual in the center span of one of the many bridges crossing the main span of the river near the city center. The sun dances along the surface of the rippling waters as far as his eye can see. Nature has a way of taking your breath away if you just stop to take notice of its many splendors.

Andrew makes his way back to his room. While looking at the sun out on the horizon from his tenth floor hotel room, he begins to realize that his situation could be so much worse and he should consider himself lucky. As he turns away from the window he notices his violin case in the corner of the room. He takes the violin out and rosins the bow. He plays *Ave Maria*, a prayer in the form of a musical masterpiece by Charles Gounod, originally written by Bach. Andrew can feel his own emotions pour out of the violin's strings as he sweeps his bow across them. Meanwhile, just outside his room, Ji-woo is pushing her room cleaning cart. She hears the music coming from Andrew's room and immediately stops to listen outside his door. She feels as if the music is pouring out of Andrew's soul. Ji-woo is deeply moved and uses a clean hand towel to wipe the tears from her eyes. She has had reservations about the truth in Andrew's alleged involvement in spying since the beginning. How could someone who is so nice and plays music with such passion be a criminal? Something just did not add up. After stalling in front of Andrews's room pretending to inventory her cart in case a manager spots her, she takes in all the music Andrew has to give and only then continues on her way wiping the remaining tears from her eyes.

Andrew puts down his violin after cleansing his soul and clearing his mind. He lays back in his bed and allows the lingering music still ringing in his ears to lull him to sleep. He wakes up in the late afternoon and decides to go out for a late lunch. The sun is warm on his face as he walks the busy streets. A woman is passing him carefully balancing a soft but bulky package on her head. Andrew smiles and bows to the woman and quickly realizes that if she bows back her package will drop from her head. Luckily the woman is non-reactive but smiles in return knowing somehow that Andrew means well. Late lunch is noodle soup today at a different small restaurant with outdoor seating. The soup is delicious and filling. After enjoying his meal he heads back out onto the streets of Seoul.

The sun is setting and Andrew wonders if Ki Young is lurking about the city. He returns to the building under construction where they met and looks for the boy but does not find him. He stays out for a few more hours and wanders around occasionally coming back to the construction site but Ki Young is nowhere to be found. Andrew knows that Ki Young can be an important ally for him so he will continue to seek him out but it's now getting dark and he will have to wait for the boy to find him. Andrew has nothing but time.

When he returns to his hotel room later in the evening he opens his door to find a piece of paper on the floor just inside his room. At first he thinks it is an invoice or notice from the hotel front desk, but as he picks it up the words he sees are handwritten by a woman and relay an unexpected message. "Coffee or tea? Please meet me at the coffee shop on Hakdong-ro 97 gil at 10 p.m." "What is this now?" Andrew asks himself out loud. He has no idea who would have left a message like this and even thinks for a minute that it may be a mistake and someone just picked the wrong door to slip the note under. After much internal deliberation and out of sheer curiosity he decides to go to the coffee shop and find out what this is all about. He gets there right at 10 p.m. since there is no worldly reason for him to be late for anything right now. He enters the small shop immediately smelling the aroma of fresh ground coffee. Scanning the room, he doesn't see anyone at first glance so he goes to the counter and orders a hot tea. Holding his tea he walks around to the back of the café and spots a single woman sitting in a booth with her back to the counter. He approaches her and as she turns her head to look at him, he instantly recognizes her smile.

10. HEART STRINGS

"Hello Mr. Andrew," states the woman. "Hello Ji-woo!" replies Andrew. "Wow, I didn't expect to find you here," he states with an astonished look on his face. "Please, sit," Ji-woo replies. "Your English is improving," Andrew comments while sitting himself down in the booth. "I am sorry but can only speak little English," she explains. In truth Ji-woo has been able to speak some English all along. She simply chooses not to reveal this ability around strange foreigners especially if she feels they are just trying to hit on her. This has always worked well for her in the past, but now she is feeling comfortable enough to open up a bit. Something is different about this man. They look at each other smiling and reach for their warm cups, simultaneously lifting them and taking a sip. Andrew wonders to himself if she has taken classes to learn some English just for him of if she has known it all along but was being cautious with him. He decides not to ask and embarrass her; besides, it did not matter since they could now understand each other. "I'm so happy to see you! Are you done working for the evening?" Andrew asks. "Yes," she replies. "Work is done." After a brief pause while staring into each other's eyes, both unable to stop smiling and occasionally lifting their cups, Ji-woo tells Andrew, "I do not believe what they say about you Mr. Andrew. I listen to your music. I like it very much. I like you also Mr. Andrew," she admits as she lowers her gaze in humility. "I like you very much also Ji-woo. Please just call me Andrew or Andy if you like," replies Andrew. "An..dy," she carefully attempts to get the pronunciation right. "Andy... I like that! Easier for me to speak," she replies.

They continue to talk to the extent possible at Ji-woo's level of understanding and Andrew himself consciously uses only simple words. He explains to her that he is not a criminal and that he has been set up. "I am innocent and I do not know why they are doing this to me. But I intend to find out and clear my name," he insists with conviction. As they continue talking, both realize that they have something in common now; neither person wants the conversation to end. They are perfectly content just being together in that small café. Ji-woo eventually tells "Andy" that she would like to show something to him. "Come for walk?" she asks. They both leave together and walk in the direction of the hotel. She shows Andrew a rear entrance to the hotel used by employees. Andrew opens the large steel door and steps up inside. He turns to Ji-woo, holding out his hand to help her inside. She hesitates only briefly before smiling and reaching out to take Andrew's hand. Her skin is soft as silk and her hand is very warm in spite of the cool night air. They walk hand in hand through the work area behind one of the restaurants.

She turns on some lights in a large dining area Andrew has not seen before. He is admiring the ambiance of the restaurant and Ji-woo's companionship as she giggles like a child pulling him around the room. They stop in front of a grand piano set on a small stage with mood lighting pouring down on it from above. "You can play, Andy?" Ji-woo asks. Andrew pulls out the seat and sits Ji-woo down on the bench. He joins her on the other side, pulls up the protective, shining keyboard cover revealing the ivory and ebony keys below. He has a look in his eyes as if he is seeing a long lost friend. He gently runs his fingers along the keys and then holds them fixed in position lowering them all at once to play a strong chord that he lets ring out and naturally decay, savoring the beauty of the rich instrument. He then looks into Ji-woo's eyes and begins to play a passage from a classical arrangement he had memorized from the past. Ji-woo looks on with a very big smile and genuine amazement.

After twenty minutes of being serenaded, Ji-woo apologizes, "I'm sorry but I must go. We can come back again." Andrew smiles and nods with affirmation. He walks with Ji-woo out of the rear entrance of the hotel. He thanks her for a wonderful evening, takes her hand up to his face and holds it against one of his cheeks. They stare at each other and while Ji-woo's face begins to mildly blush, she quickly leans into him and kisses him on the other cheek. She slowly pulls her hand back and turns to walk away. Andrew can only watch and does not even blink until she is out of sight. He can feel his heart beating again only much stronger. He leans back against a wall for support and savors the moments that highlighted his night and indeed his entire life. Something has changed in Andrew and he can feel it now for the first time.

Walking on a cloud, he returns to the hotel and walks into the lobby, bows to the front desk staff and heads up to his room. Nothing can top this day so he gives up on the idea of doing anything else but playing a little more music. While playing soft melodies he eyes his cassette recorders and gets an idea. With the first recorder he can record only a single track of music. But with two recorders he can record a second track on the second recorder while playing along with the first recorder's playback audio. In other words, he can create multitrack recordings having two cassette player/recorders. Smiling, he realizes that he can start recording his own music now and he knows just who will appreciate his first recording. "This is brilliant!" he says out loud. "Why didn't I think of this before?" He will need access to the piano to start out so he decides to wait for his next chance meeting with Ji-woo. He is so excited now that it is difficult for him to contain it. He turns on the TV for the first time in a long time and watches a drama without turning the volume down. Halfway through he scans the channels and realizes that the news story about him has stopped airing. Laying back in bed, he falls asleep with the Korean program still flickering on the TV.

The next morning he pulls open the curtains to reveal the sunrise, hops in the shower and goes down for breakfast. He finally decides it is time to suggest to the chef that the eggs would both look and taste better if they were cooked just a little longer. The chef agrees and promises to make the change starting with Andrew's breakfast this morning. He brings out some scrambled eggs and personally delivers them to Andrew. Andrew picks up his fork, takes a mouthful and smiles with satisfaction giving the chef a big thumbs-up. "Why didn't I just do this before?" Andrew says under his breath after the cook returns to the kitchen. "Such a small change can have such a large impact on starting a day," he thinks to himself. After breakfast Andrew heads out for a long walk and only stops to take in the beauty of the river's reflection of the rising sun. Everything beautiful in nature now reminds him of Ji-woo and her smile.

He doesn't want to stop walking and ends up roaming the streets for the rest of the morning and half of the afternoon. At dinner Ji-woo is working back at the hotel so he eats there just to be able to see her again. They both realize Andrew's predicament so their interactions in public are self-restrained and are limited to pleasantries and subdued smiles. After dinner Andrew takes the bill folder, puts the cost on his room, tips Ji-woo and slips in a note for her eyes only. She rings up the bill and stashes the note in her pocket until she can look at it later when she has privacy. "Coffee or tea? Please meet me. 10 p.m. Andy," she whispers under her breath while reading the note on her break. She holds the note close to her heart, closes her eyes slowly and lets out a long sigh. She then giggles like a young school child as she hurries back into work.

Later that evening she finds Andrew sitting at the same bench near the end wall of the café. This time his back faces the café counter. He has already ordered them both a hot beverage. They talk for hours. She finds him comical and in the beginning tries to contain her laughter. But as time goes on she lets down her guard. They are simply in the moment, finding joy in each other's company. When they decide to leave, Andrew asks if he could possibly play the piano in the restaurant again. Ji-woo, with delight in her eyes says, "Yes, please play for me."

They find themselves seated at the piano in the dimly lit room again. Side by side, Andrew plays music while singing to Ji-woo. He tries to get her to sing along, but she shies away from his request saying, "The last thing you want to hear is me singing!" After what feels both like a lifetime and a completely timeless moment, she suggests that they should go. Andrew takes out a cassette recorder from his coat pocket and places it on the piano. He says softly to her, "Just one more song." He presses the record button and begins playing the piano part to *Ave Maria*. When he is done he stops the recorder and he notices Ji-woo is on the verge of tearing up. They hug each other tightly and stand up very slowly unable to break their gaze. Andrew places the recorder back in his pocket and walks Ji-woo to their usual departure point. She begs him for a copy of the tape but he tells her it is not finished yet and goes on to describe how patience is a virtue. "I don't agree," she replies. "But I will wait."

Andrew takes Ji-woo's hand and pulls her closer to him. They tightly hug each other once again as Andrew thanks Ji-woo for being here for him. While still embracing each other, Ji-woo looks Andrew straight in the eyes and sees a reflection of honesty, real gratitude and the shimmering moonlight. Their lips meet in a release of passion that has been building slowly for weeks. Afterward, they hold each other even more tightly than before. Ji-woo's eyes begin to well up with emotion too strong for her to retain. They are tears of joy. They linger awhile longer holding each other until Ji-woo kisses him once again and pulls his hair back to take one last look deep into his eyes. She then smiles, turns around and walks away pausing only briefly to look back at the building light shining down on Andrew who is unable to take his eyes off her. After a fleeting moment she is gone. Andrew is feeling his own emotions course through his veins. He stares up at the stars and begins to thank each one of them he can see piercing through the city lights. Ji-woo is now a vision that guides him and gives him both purpose and the drive he will need to right everything that is wrong in his life.

Time has stopped for Andrew but time also has a way of rebooting itself. He finds himself back in his room staring at the tape recorder he took from his jacket with the *Ave Maria* recording. He sits down in an easy chair, pulls out his violin and rosins up the bow. He then arranges the second recorder estimating the proper distance and volume from the first. He then presses the play button on the piano recording while simultaneously pressing the record button on the second recorder with a blank tape. He begins playing along with the piano and is recording a virtual duet. His eyes are closed as music pours out of his soul like water cascading down a waterfall. When he is done he realizes that his own eyes have teared up as he reaches for the stop buttons on both recorders. There will be no second take. He puts his instrument away and lays back on his bed, pulling a spare pillow to his chest and wrapping his arms around it. His eyes close slowly as a sense of peace leads him into a deep sleep.

11. A PATH IN THE PARK

After the best rest he has gotten in ages, Andrew goes through his morning routine with a little bounce in his step. Thanks to his relationship with Ji-woo he finds himself in a state of acceptance that brings him peace and a renewed sense of appreciation for life. The day flies by as he goes about his usual business of not doing any business at all. Occasionally thoughts of his former life back in the US bubble up to the surface but they dissolve as quickly as they arise. The irony of his situation and him now living an adventure he has always dreamed about makes him laugh to himself. "I should be careful what I wish for," he tells himself.

He knows that Ji-woo is working at the hotel restaurant this evening so he plans to eat dinner there just to be near her. She greets him after he is seated and although they use great discretion about their relationship in public, they intensely enjoy being in each other's presence. After his meal Andrew takes the bill folder, takes care of the meal and tip and also slips his finished cassette tape recording inside for Ji-woo. She peeks inside briefly, smiles and bounces up and down enthusiastically. She informs him in a whisper that she will be unable to meet him later since she will be visiting her parents for the weekend, but promises to listen to the tape as soon as she gets out of work. She caresses Andrew's hands before he gets up to leave. "I will see you again soon, but not soon enough for me," she tells him. He smiles and bows in respect to her before he heads for the door. He has to fight his own urge to turn around and run back to her.

Andrew goes outside to take in some fresh air. The night air is cool but still. Walking the streets has become a form of meditation for him and he doesn't feel right if he skips out on it. He wanders around again just letting his feet go where they want to guide him. There is a park where cherry blossoms are in full bloom now. The city lights are bright enough to illuminate the richly colored blossoms and the scent of the delicate petals perfume the air. He sits on one of the park benches to relax when a voice calls out to him from behind, "Hello Mr. Andrew." It's Ki Young's voice that Andrew immediately recognizes. "Hello Ki Young. Come and sit," he urges the boy. After they are seated and exchange some small talk, Ki Young tells Andrew some news. "My full name is Ki Young Kwon. My father works for our government," the boy methodically explains. "I thought that if anyone could prove that you are innocent, it would be him. I visited his office and although he was in a meeting, I looked around while I was waiting for him. I decided to get into his e-mail account to see if your name was mentioned anywhere." "How did you do that?" Andrew asks. "Let's just say I like computers and am very good with them since I was introduced to them right after I was born. In fact, I can do tricks with my smart phone like a magician pulls rabbits out of his hat," Ki young continues. "Anyway, once I accessed my father's e-mail account, I did a filtered search for anything with your name in the title or text. Dozens of emails popped up. I am sorry for what I am about to say to you and it brings me great embarrassment. I didn't want to believe it at first, but my father knows that you are innocent and now I know the truth. He is working with your own government to keep you here and silence you. You were right when you told me you were set up. They planted evidence against you in your room. I always saw my father as a good man but he has brought my family dishonor. I cannot ignore the truth, Mr. Andrew." Ki Young lowers his head in shame. Andrew responds and pulls Ki Young's face back up, gently lifting his chin, "Thank you Ki Young. Try not to blame your father and feel bad. Grown-ups are sometimes forced to do things they know are wrong but they have no choice. I'm sure your father has a good heart deep down inside. We are all good souls. After all, he made you and you are the noblest young man I have ever met." Ki Young looks at Andrew with a restrained smile and replies, "Well this is still not right and we need to do something about it. I would like you to meet a friend of mine. He is one of our most respected elders and can move mountains. He will have the wisdom to guide you. You will need his help."

Ki Young takes out his smart phone and his little finger scribbles out a shape that acts as a password. He opens an application on his phone that detects strong broadcasting signals and scans Andrew's body from chest down in sweeping motions. "Empty your pockets please," Ki Young requests. After scanning the contents of Andrew's pockets, Ki Young lifts up the hotel key Andrew has been using to access his room. "This key is bugged!" Ki exclaims. "This is no ordinary plastic key card. They must have an RFID chip in it. They know where you are right now. You can't get rid of it because they will find out and you will not be able to get back in your room. Come, there is a tree with a hollow where we can put it for now. We will come back for it later."

Ki Young leads Andrew through the park where they stash the bugged key and then brings him to a Buddhist temple situated right in the middle of the busy city. Ki Young explains that it is over 1200 years old. They put some money in a box and light a candle, placing it on a stone altar among two dozen other candles that are at various stages of burning down. He then takes Andrew to a large meditation room that is lined with miniature golden statues. There must be thousands of them. Both Andrew and Ki Young remove their shoes and walk around to the back of the room where Andrew spots a man sitting with his legs crossed and appears to be in a deep meditative state. Andrew has seen this man before. He is the vendor who sells sweet potatoes in the street! Ki Young instructs Andrew to sit on an empty mat just behind the man as Ki Young sits down also. "Close your eyes and meditate," instructs the boy. After a minute or so of silence, Ki Young begins whispering in Korean to the elder in front of them. The elder responds and each time Ki Young translates for Andrew. "We are a good people," Ki Young begins translating. "Do not hold anger in your heart as it will injure your spirit. The truth is like the light from a strong star. The light of day hides the starlight but the setting sun allows everyone to see the shining star once again. One has only to look up to find that the star has always been there. You must follow your shining star of truth wherever it leads you. This is your destiny Mr. Trainor." Andrew speaks and Ki Young translates. "I thought for a time that destiny forgot about me and left me behind but I am now following a newly lit path. This path feels good to me but somehow it must lead me out of the darkness where I have been for so long." The elder responds, "Believe in your true self. The truth will shine its light on our people and you will be free and left alone to make choices. Please make these choices with an open heart and you will always be at peace with the life you create. We will do whatever we can to help you. I am Jong-su and I am your humble servant. Please visit me again when you want to meditate or taste more sweet potato." "Thank you for your wisdom Jong-su. I am in your debt," replies Andrew as Ki Young signals that it is time to go.

Before they walk together back to the hollowed tree, Andrew stops to thank Ki Young for introducing him to Jong-su. "I would like to see more of the temple before we leave if that's OK," asks Andrew. The boy agrees but he has little time, so he explains that they will have to be quick. Ki Young brings Andrew to every part of the temple compound and explains the meaning behind the statues, sacred pictures and ancient burial sites. The temple seems to be out of place amidst all of the tall, modern buildings and one would think it would be a better fit on a mountaintop. However, in retrospect, it occurs to Andrew that it's really the tall buildings that are out of place while standing in the serenity of the temple. Ki Young brings

Andrew back to the park where they retrieve his bugged room key. "I obviously know your hotel since it's written on the key card but what is your room number? I might need to find you in a hurry one day," Ki Young asks Andrew. "1005 on the tenth floor," Andrew replies. "You will like the view, but don't show up unannounced like my mother would until I have a chance to clean the place up. Besides, I might have a girlfriend inside," Andrews says with a big grin. Ki Young rolls his eyes and shakes his head as he responds, "A girlfriend? You sure know how to find trouble. In fact, you are an expert on trouble and should write a book about it!" Andrew laughs and thanks Ki Young once again as they head off in separate directions. At a few dozen steps apart Ki Young turns around and asks Andrew if he was serious about the girl. Andrew replies that he met a girl at the hotel. "Her name is Ji-woo," Andrew shouts out. "Her name is trouble!" Ki Young replies and can still be seen shaking his head as he disappears into the night. Andrew meditates on the events of the evening and the words from Jong-su. He is convinced that Jong-su never opened his eyes the entire time they were together. His body also never moved and was as still as the hand carved jade Buddha statue overlooking the city from the temple.

Andrew is now walking on a different cloud as peace fills each and every cell of his body. It occurs to him that time alone does not heal all wounds, but it is the body's allotment of time that permits healing to take place within. Andrew's mind, having reached total acceptance, is now beginning to heal. Before he knows it he is looking up at his room from the outside of the hotel. Both the hotel and his room are looking less like a prison and more like a home for him. He makes his way to his room and attempts to meditate for a few moments. He is then inspired to take out some sheet music, pick up his violin and practice for a while. He plays his heart out with renewed energy and vigor.

After finishing a beautiful piece of music he puts his violin down and shuffles through his music sheets for a specific song he is inspired to play. While setting the music sheets in place he happens to glance out the hotel window at a brightly lit Korean business sign that catches his eye. Of course he is still unable to read the text but he finds himself staring deeply into the Korean characters. Something is happening to those characters in Andrew's brain; they are becoming increasingly vibrant and a pattern is emerging. The pattern is very familiar to him although he cannot figure out why. He involuntarily looks back at his music sheets for a moment as if someone unseen is turning his head. He quickly looks back out the window at the Korean text again and it is then that Andrew experiences a moment of absolute epiphany. His mind has projected and overlaid a musical staff perfectly aligned over the text characters on the side of the building. This happens very faintly in the beginning but the staff overlay becomes more and more prominent as the seconds tick away. Finally, in a single pivotal moment, Andrew sees sections of the Korean text morph before his own eyes into musical notes on the scale. He is unable to stop staring at this phenomena and the mirage is not going away either. He is seeing actual music that was previously hidden inside the Korean text. Impulsively, he picks up a small notepad that the hotel provides and quickly draws out a rough musical staff using a hotel menu edge like a ruler to make straight lines. He then looks back at the sign and copies onto the staff the characters in the same perfect alignment that he can still plainly see in his mind. Using a marker, he then highlights the morphed music notes within the characters onto the staff in their proper place. He sits back and stares repeatedly back and forth at the notepad drawing and the sign outside. Andrew is stunned.

He picks up his violin and plays the transposed and unique combination of notes and to his amazement, they make musical sense. They are actually the beginning notes of a potential song! In excitement that he is unable to contain he quickly grabs his coat, notepad and pen and races outside to the streets below. He briskly walks to the restaurant next door to the hotel that has another brightly lit advertising sign spelled out with Korean characters. He stares at it and almost instantaneously he sees the musical notes come to life on the sign over his visualized musical scale backdrop. He feverishly scribbles down the text on a fresh page of the notepad and keeps moving down the street capturing sign text as he goes. Almost without exception Andrew is finding music in plain view embedded into the Korean language that has remained hidden from both himself and an entire nation of people looking at and using it every day. With all of his energy and notepad pages spent, he turns around and brings his musical harvest back to his room. Tearing each single page off the notebook, he lays them one by one them across his bed sheets and steps back to fully appreciate the totality of his discovery. His mood lightens as he realizes that he's going to need more paper and a bigger bed.

He goes back to the first musical script he put on paper, picks it up and places it where he can see it over the body of his violin. He plays the handful of notes on the page and stops when they end to savor the feeling they evoke in him. He repeats this process over and over again until the pace and feel of the song sets into his mind. Like riding a bicycle for the first time as a youth, Andrew gains a sense of balance after just a few "pedals" and the rest of the song materializes effortlessly. His last run through this initial handful of notes does not stop, but continues with a life and will of its own. Having run out of paper he quickly sets up one of his cassette players and hits the record button. His eyes are closed as he plays this piece again and completely lets go, allowing the music to move through him like the air he breathes; effortless and nourishing.

Andrew stops to play the recording back and repeatedly listens to it in amazement. Something inside him refuses to claim responsibility for the sheer beauty of the work. He sees himself as simply a vehicle bringing to light this music that has laid dormant since the inception of this ancient language. He is also about to make his first openhearted choice in life; he will follow this new musical path no matter where it takes him. His excitement does not waver but only increases as he picks up the second scribbled text of street sign notes on the hotel notepaper and repeats the same process. The second song is as beautiful and melodic as the first but is also uniquely different. Andrew is unable to stop himself from unlocking this secret music until he realizes that it is now six o'clock in the morning and he has been going all night without food or sleep. He forces himself to stop, clears off his bed and lays himself down to rest. As the quietness settles over him, it occurs to Andrew that his entire life has been one long unheard song in the making. The new music, still echoing in his mind, softly lulls him to sleep.

12. A NEW DAY

After sleeping through the morning and into early afternoon Andrew wakes up and looks out across his room at the sunshine lighting up the collection of papers, the recorders and his violin sitting against the easy chair. He smiles to himself and says, "Thank God it was real and not a dream." Feeling hungry, he washes up, gets dressed and heads down to one of the lobby restaurants for food. He picks up one of the lobby magazines from the rack and takes it with him for his late breakfast. While eating he flips through the magazine written of course entirely in Korean, only this time he is more interested in the text than the pictures. Again, he now only sees music in the written characters on the pages. He thinks back on his visit to the old Buddhist temple in the center of the city and wonders what kind of music he would find in the ancient sacred scriptures housed and protected there. Without a doubt it would have to be some of the most beautiful music ever heard. Andrew decides that he will have to go back to the temple and find the music within those holy

CHARLES MICHAEL LANDRY

words, some of which are over one thousand years old, and bring that music to life. He will need Ki Young to escort him back there again so he will need to wait for that opportunity.

The rest of the day is spent taking his walks and returning to make more music in his room. After filling a few cassette tapes with music, he realizes that he is going to need more blank tapes. He will pick more up when he is out on another one of his long walks around the markets. The day turns into night as he transposes an endless flow of musical notation onto blank printer paper he has "borrowed" from the hotel lobby office printer. Once he sees the written music on paper he begins to compose the accompanying piano parts that will be recorded at his next opportunity in front of the piano. By the time he has the accompanying piano notation for the solo violin music he has composed, it is after midnight and Andrew realizes that time is both ceasing to exist and simultaneously flying by. He decides to rearrange the furniture in the room to make space on the floor to lay out and organize his written music. Sheets of music cover almost the entire carpet. He lays back in bed and angles his head on the pillow to view the staggering amount of music composition that lay before him like a blanket of freshly fallen white flower petals. While reflecting back on his life he becomes aware that never before has his life had such intense meaning. Even if no one ever sees or hears this music he is creating, Andrew feels a sense of complete satisfaction in this work. This is his last thought before he drifts off to sleep.

He wakes up the following morning realizing the weekend has ended and that means Ji-woo will be back.

He is as excited about this as he is about his musical discovery. He quickly goes through his morning routine and heads out for breakfast. Although Andrew forgets the specifics of Ji-woo's schedule besides the evening restaurant hours, she has been assigned to clean rooms for the morning and this includes the tenth floor.

After cleaning a dozen rooms, she reaches the front of Andrew's room. She is greeted by a small boy walking through the hallway. The boy stops in front of Andrew's room also and stares at Ji-woo intensely. After seeing her name tag he exclaims, "So, you are Ji-woo!" She is quite surprised by his unexpected comment. "How do you know my name?" she asks. "It's written on your name tag," Ki Young responds. "Besides, Andrew has told me about you. Maybe he is just crazy anyway but he certainly seems to be crazy about you." Ji-woo realizes that she can converse in Korean with the boy and asks him his name. "Ki Young, and I am Andrew's friend," he replies.

"I need to work now. Can we speak while I clean Andrew's room? You should not be with me but I absolutely must speak with you," Ji-woo remarks as she unlocks Andrew's hotel door after repeatedly knocking with no reply. "I don't think my friend will mind, but he did warn me about his room," Ki Young states. They both walk through the door and are immediately equally fixated on the sheer volume of written music covering the floor of Andrew's room. "I told you he was crazy!" Ki Young exclaims. Ji-woo replies, "He is not crazy at all. He is a beautiful artist and I have heard him play myself. You cannot appreciate just how good he is Ki Young." The boy has his back to Ji-woo as he closely examines a cassette tape with music on it. When she calls his name he quickly turns around with the tape kept out of view behind his back. As she speaks to him he gently slips the tape into his pocket without her perception. Ji-woo sits Ki Young down on the easy chair and begs him to tell her everything he knows about Andrew. "So, let me get this right; you are crazy about him too?" inquires the boy. Ji-woo just smiles. Ki Young then begins to tell Ji-woo how he and Andrew met and everything he knows about Andrew and his innocence. After a twenty minute conversation Ji-woo gives Ki Young a big hug and thanks him repeatedly. "I am happy to help my friend Andrew. Just please don't hug me like that again. I do need to breathe you know!" Ki Young exclaims. Ji-woo apologizes and leads the boy to the door. Before he leaves he turns to her one more time and hands her a sealed envelope. "Please open this later when you are alone. You will know what to do with it. I don't know why I am even doing this, really I don't," remarks Ki Young.

Ki Young heads off down the hallway shaking his head in disbelief and Ji-woo returns to Andrew's room and tries to make up his bed without disturbing any of his paperwork covering the floor. She quickly completes cleaning his room and supplying fresh linens before she closes his door and heads off down the hallway. She continues her work for the rest of the morning with both the sealed envelope and the sheet music in Andrew's room weighing heavy on her mind. When she is finally done with her morning work, she changes out of her cleaning staff uniform and heads outside to a coffee shop for a tea and a peek at the contents of the envelope.

Inside the envelope is a small stack of paper copies of emails. They capture conversations discussing in detail the plot designed to set Andrew up and trap him in Seoul, preventing him from revealing the real US covert operation he discovered. The exchanges between the Korean intelligence officer and the Tilton Global Corporation official include bank account numbers and agreed payoff amounts. These emails can be conclusive evidence supporting Andrew's innocence. Ji-woo is elated at the idea of holding in her hands the key to Andrew's freedom and finally knowing the truth beyond question. Yet moments later she is filled with melancholy at the prospect of Andrew leaving Korea and herself behind if he were to board a plane and return home to America a free man. Still she decides that revealing the truth and clearing the name of an innocent man is a greater cause than her own desires. She will do the right thing.

In the meantime, Ki Young has returned home and once he is alone in his bedroom he takes out the cassette tape with Andrew's recorded music on it and places it into his stereo system, puts his headphones on and presses the play button. As the music begins to play, his eyes close and he lies back in his chair to fully focus on the music. He is deeply moved with emotion brought out in part by the beauty of the music and also in part by the realization of his father's wrong doing. Tears fill his eyes when the song ends and he pulls off his head phones. He remembers the words of Jong-su in the temple and he agrees that the Koreans are a good people. He also thinks that they deserve to hear this beautiful music Andrew has composed and, after careful consideration, he decides that it would be a personal tribute to Andrew for him to post the music on social media sites rather than letting it sit in a drawer in Andrew's hotel room. He goes right to work taking the cassette audio and converting it to MP3 format making it Internet-ready. He then posts it on various blogs and media sites on the web anonymously but pointing out who the composer is and speaking in generalities to his innocence. Within minutes of the postings, people are enthusiastically responding in droves. Most are deeply moved and comment on the sheer beauty of the compositions. Ki Young sits back and watches the postings starting to go viral in front of his very eyes. With his father's actions still weighing heavy on his mind, he finds some comfort in seeing the positive reactions of his people on the web. "I'll be happy after the first million hits on these sites," he says to himself softly.

Later in the day, Andrew returns to the hotel, drops off some blank cassette tapes in his room and heads down for dinner to see Ji-woo. Once seated at his table he ignores the menu and keeps a lookout for Ji-woo. She finally comes out of the kitchen with a food order held high on a tray and she displays an expression of exuberant happiness when she spots Andrew. As soon as she is able, she goes directly to his table and tells him how happy she is to see him. She takes Andrew's order but asks him to limit his meal because she would like to take him out to dinner after she is done working. "It will only be a few more hours if you can wait that long. I want to take you somewhere special. I am so excited and we have so much to talk about!" she exclaims. "That's great! I have news too and I've missed you so much!" Andrew replies. It's obvious to him that she is beginning to throw some of her caution to the wind since she is much more open, showing her affection during their interactions during dinner. Andrew is loving every minute of it.

She tells Andrew to meet her outside the hotel just after 10 p.m. When she comes around from the rear of the building, he is there waiting for her with a huge smile and a very warm embrace. They walk off together down the busy street and in the excitement that neither one of them can contain, they both start speaking at once blurting out news they each have been dying to share. Ji-woo immediately realizes that they are talking over each other and not really listening and she pauses to laugh out loud. She gently places her finger over Andrew's lips while he is still talking and he looks her in the eyes and begins to laugh also. She says, "OK, my news can wait. Please start from the beginning and tell me everything." Andrew tells Ji-woo about his discovery of the music he finds hidden in the Korean language. He goes on to tell her that he has been swept away with finding, composing and recording this music all weekend. "The angels have brought you to me and I can honestly say that you have saved my life, but the angels had another gift in store for me. They opened my eyes so that I could see the music that is hidden in plain sight in your native language. I have pages and pages of music that comes directly from Korean text hanging on ordinary street signs up and down this road." Ji-woo is in awe of what Andrew has just described and at first thinks that it could not be possible. "I have read these signs and spoken this language my entire life and no one I know has ever proposed such an idea. How do you see music in our written text? Can you show me?" Ji-woo begs of Andrew. He immediately asks her to stop walking and turn around to face a building that has a restaurant sign they can both see and Andrew can reach with his hands. He then draws out the imaginary lines of the music notation with his fingers over the length of the sign until she understands the concept and can hold the thought of the lines in her mind. He then points out where the musical notes are and even sings them out loud for her. A sudden look of realization comes over Ji-woo's face. "This is actually real. I can see it myself now! Oh my God! All of this time and in fact all of time as I know it, this music has been sitting here waiting for you. It is heaven who has sent you to us Andy" Ji-woo responds as her eyes begin to tear up. "You must let me hear this music!" she begs of him. "Oh, you will," Andrew replies. "You are my only audience!"

"What's your news then?" he inquires as they continue their walk down the street. Ji-woo responds that it is very important but can wait until they are at the restaurant. "I'm still trying to absorb what you have just revealed to me," she says. They walk arm in arm as she studies Andrew's face and is unable to stop staring at him. He is trying to keep his eyes on the walkway so they don't walk into a pole or fall off the curb, but he frequently turns to her and smiles. Each time their eyes lock, Ji-woo looks deeply inside him, searching her own soul and turning her female intuition up to full scale in order to establish if the man she is falling in love with is actually real. She has never met another man like him. While they walk along a winding side road, Andrew tells Ji-woo about his visit to the Buddhist temple in the city center. He also tells her about his burning desire to see the sacred writings housed in the temple. "Imagine the music I could find in the holy writings. It would have to be as divine and spiritually uplifting as the meaning of the words themselves. I just know it," he says. "Then we will go there. I will bring you there tomorrow myself," Ji-woo replies.

They arrive at a very old traditional Korean restaurant that resembles one of the curved roof houses and pagoda-style homes seen throughout the older parts of the city. "This restaurant is very famous and is one of my favorite places in the city. You will love it," Ji-woo tells Andrew. "Do they have kimchi?" Andrew asks. "Yes, of course. Every place has kimchi!" she says while laughing and opening the front door. As soon as Andrew steps inside the restaurant, a sense of peace settles upon him. Maybe it's the feng shui design of the interior and the bamboo plants inviting you in like a secret garden or it's the gently bowing staff dressed in old traditional Korean style garments welcoming them inside. Whatever it is, he feels very comfortable and understands why Ji-woo likes this place so much. After some suggestions from Ji-woo in Korean, the hostess walks them to a quiet area in the back of the restaurant. Andrew finds himself looking at the décor and a very old looking shelved nook where various pieces of pottery are displayed. The pottery looks handmade and looks to be very old. When they arrive at their table Ji-woo tells Andrew that he must remove his shoes. The table is very low to the floor and they will be sitting on cushions. "I love this!" Andrew admits to Ji-woo. She smiles and replies, "I was hoping you would say that. I eat here with my family on special occasions when they come to visit me in Seoul. They live far from here in a small village in the mountains." "I wish I could visit there. It sounds very beautiful. Your parents must be as adorable as you are. I would like to meet them someday. I guess I have to find a way out of the mess I'm in first," Andrew replies.

As they remove their shoes and sit down in the candlelit space, Ji-woo responds, "I may be able to help you with that." She orders food from the waitress for herself and Andrew as he sits quietly watching her face glowing in the candlelight while wondering what she could have meant by that statement. After the waitress leaves, Ji-woo begins to tell Andrew how she met Ki Young at the hotel (although she leaves out the part about them both being in his room) and that he left her evidence proving that Andrew had been framed. She explains, "I brought copies of the e-mail evidence to the press in Seoul. I hope you do not mind. I thought it would be less trouble for you this way. By tomorrow everyone in my country will know the truth about you. I can only pray that our government officials do the right thing and release you giving you your freedom back. I have to admit that I am also praying that once you regain your freedom, you do not leave me. Now that I have found you I do not want to imagine my life without you in it." She lowers her head after her last statement. Andrew is absolutely stunned by Ji-woo's news of the e-mail evidence but realizes that this miraculous news pales in comparison to their mutual feelings toward each other at this moment. He reaches for her hands and tugs them gently toward him encouraging her to lift her eyes back up to meet his own as he replies, "Leaving you is unthinkable and not an option. Because of you I feel my own heart beating and know I have a soul. No matter what happens, it will happen to the both of us because without you, I am nothing," Ji-woo wipes the tears from her eyes and lunges over the table falling into

Andrew's open arms as they tightly embrace, neither one of them wanting to let go. "I love you," she whispers in his ear while still locked in his arms. They are both smiling and tearing up at the same time as Andrew replies, "And I will never stop loving you Ji-woo."

13. MUSIC IN THE AIR

During dinner at the restaurant, beautiful music begins to play and Andrew looks all around but cannot find the source. "What is that?" he asks Ji-woo. "It is a woman playing the gayageum. It is a Korean zither and is similar to a stringed harp," she replies. "It is amazingly beautiful and graceful," Andrew responds as he takes Ji-woo's hand and they search for the musician. Now with a female musician and the gayageum in full view, Andrew is mesmerized by both the sound it makes and the finger movements of the artist. Ji-woo whispers in Andrew's ear that the instrument is a traditional Korean instrument dating back in time to the sixth century during a period called the Gaya Confederacy. "The strings are made from silk," she says as Andrew looks at her with an expression of surprise. "Silk?" he asks. "Not catgut or metal?" "What is catgut?" Ji-woo asks as she tugs on Andrew's sleeve indicating that they should return to their table. "In the old days, they used to make violin strings from the inside parts of cats. I won't go into specifics since we are eating. I don't even know how they made the strings. I just remember playing on them when I was young," Andrew explains and continues, "I really wish I could get that instrument on one of my recordings. It's so beautiful." "Speaking of beautiful recordings, can I return with you to the hotel and listen to the music you are stealing from our language?" Ji-woo asks with a sly grin. "Of course!" he replies, "I'm ready when you are."

They finish their meal and Andrew takes out some money but she refuses to let him pay saying, "Please. Silence is golden! You can return the favor when you are famous." As they pass the woman musician on the way out, Andrew places a tip on the table for her and takes one of her business cards. "What could you possibly do with that business card? You can't even read it!" Ji-woo inquires. "Maybe I could get her to join my band," Andrew replies with a big grin on his face. They head off arm in arm again, lazily making their way back towards the hotel. Ji-woo's cell phone begins to ring and she quickly apologizes to Andrew and answers the call. She is conversing in Korean on the phone and is beginning to sound very excited. "This is my sister," she whispers to Andrew as she continues to carry on with varying expressions on her face that border on mild shock. When the conversation is over and she puts the phone away, she explains to Andrew, "Ki Young has put your music on the Internet. Please don't be angry. It is most likely my fault. And my sister said that your music is now going viral. Millions of people are listening to it right now and are talking about it non-stop. They somehow know the truth already and love your songs. I also explained to my sister where your inspiration comes from and she could not believe it either. She told me that she was going to post that on the web herself because people really need to know about this." "I don't know what to say. Believe me when I say that I am not angry at all but is this a good thing? Will this help us?" Andrew asks. "Of course it will help us! The people here are very caring and have very kind hearts. With our people on your side, you have already won your cause. I'm just jealous because I am the only one who has not heard your new music yet," Ji-woo laments. "Well, we will fix that right now," Andrew insists. "Let's go."

They reach the hotel and Ji-woo walks Andrew very intentionally right through the front door, through the lobby and greets the front desk staff as they head for the elevator. The staff can be seen in the background behind them whispering to each other with inquisitive looks on their faces. They reach the door of Andrew's room and he turns to Ji-woo asking if it would be alright for them to take the music and recorders from his room to the piano again since he wants to do some more recording if possible. She replies to him, "I've made arrangements with the restaurant manager. You can use the piano anytime you want. There is no problem. You have gone from victim to VIP now!" she exclaims. "OK, then I can do that later. Please come in," he says as he slowly opens the door hoping the room is clean and not a disaster. She sits down on the edge of the bed after they remove their coats. Andrew takes out one of the recorders, selects a tape to play and inserts it. He then hands Ji-woo a set of headphones he had bought some time ago and asks her to put them on. He then presses the play button and sits back in his easy chair watching the expressions on Ji-woo's face. She is moved to tears. When the song is over, she takes off the headphones and places them in her lap and speaks slowly, "I have never been so touched by such a beautiful piece of music. No wonder people are talking about it. When I close my eyes and listen to this music, I feel like I am surrounded by heaven. God has sent you to me. Maybe he has really sent you to our people and I just happen to be in the way or was the one who made first eye contact with you." "Ji-woo, as much as I would like to take credit for this music, I feel I am just a messenger. This music was here all along hidden but waiting to be discovered. I just stumbled on it first," Andrew replies. "You're too modest," Ji-woo comments.

Andrew takes Ji-woo by the hand and helps her up as she hands him back the headphones. They stand face to face looking deep into each other's eyes and after a few moments Andrew asks if he can go with her someday to meet her parents at their home in the mountains. She responds, "I would like that very much. They will love you." Ji-woo then takes off her shoes, picks up the recorder, unplugs the headphones, presses the play button and turns the volume down to a pleasant level. She then dims the light, lays back in Andrew's bed with her head snuggling into a pillow and asks Andrew if she could stay a while longer and enjoy the music. He asks her, "Do you have to go at all?" She replies in a whisper as she pulls Andrew's body down next to her, "I don't know. I might just be far too busy to drag myself away from here tonight." She displays the same sly grin as before and they embrace each other holding on for dear life in a long and passionate kiss. Tonight, in Andrew's room, it will only be the night that fades.

THE SOUNDS OF SILENCE

Morning comes too soon for the loving couple. Ji-woo begs Andrew not to look at her as she races for the bathroom to fix her hair and freshen up. "I probably look like a monster," she shouts out from the bath. "Why is it that men just look sexy in the morning with tossed hair and women look like they have turned into pumpkins?" she inquires. "But you are my beautiful pumpkin. You don't realize that you are even more beautiful waking up next to me with the morning sun lighting up your face," Andrew replies. Still in the bathroom, she fires back, "Great! So you're telling me I had a spotlight on my monster face. That's just perfect!" Andrew cannot hold back his laughter as he insists, "You're too modest!" "Touché," Ji-woo responds. She races out of the bathroom and quickly kisses Andrew stating as she turns for the door, "I'm late for work but you were worth it." "You'll know where to find me," Andrew says in parting as she slips out the door and he slowly closes it savoring the moment. "If I could paint, I'm sure I could paint her from memory right now," he says softly to himself as he heads back into his room.

After his morning routine, he goes down for breakfast and then goes out for a power walk. It's not a real power walk in the sense of a brisk, rapid-paced exercise but it is a casual long walk that recharges his batteries. Just being out in the morning sunshine and admiring the flowers and trees makes the tall buildings fade into the background. There is really only one thing on his mind and her smile is what he yearns for now. As he crosses the road and begins walking down a side street, he is approached by an older woman. The woman recognizes him from the news reports and realizes that this is the man

101

making the music everyone is talking about. "Excuse me. I just want to comment on your music. My kids played it for me on their computer thing or whatever it is. You are very talented and your music is the most beautiful thing I have ever heard. I also understand what has happened to you. Please trust that things will resolve themselves and please, please keep making your music. I wish you the best." She walks off and leaves Andrew quite surprised by her comments. A reinforcing sense of pride follows him on his continued walk.

It is about mid-afternoon by the time he returns back to the hotel. When he opens the door of his hotel room he sees a small plant on the office desk. It's a bonsai tree. There is a note peeking out from underneath it. He pulls out the note and reads it, immediately recognizing Ji-woo's handwriting:

"I have managed to take several days off from work. Would you like to accompany me to my parents' house in the mountains? I think the authorities will not bother you. We can hide your key and it will only be for a few days anyway. I think you need to see more trees and less buildings. Pack a few things and be ready to leave tonight. I'll come get you. Luv, Ji."

Andrew does not even hesitate and begins to load up his backpack. The thought of being in the mountains and not just staring at them from a distance is a thrilling proposition. Also, being with Ji-woo and stepping outside of his ten block cell for any period of time is an equally thrilling proposition. He has one more thing in mind that he would like to accomplish before he leaves the city; he would like to visit the temple and study the sacred scriptures. He will ask Ji-woo if this is possible.

14. ROAD TRIP

Ji-woo knocks on Andrew's door at nightfall. He opens the door with his backpack over his shoulder and they immediately embrace each other and kiss. "I take it you want to go with me then," she says as she laughs at Andrew's eagerness. "I wouldn't miss this for the world," Andrew responds. "Wait. Please give me your key," Ji-woo insists. She opens his door and slips the key back into the power saver slot that keeps the lights turned on in the room. She also hangs the "Do Not Disturb" sign on the outside door handle and closes the door tight. "How am I going to get back in?" Andrew asks. "With my key, of course. Remember, I clean these rooms so I have a master key. Besides, no one will know you are gone this way," Ji-woo replies. "You, my little pumpkin, are a genius! Can I call you pumpkin?" Andrew asks as they begin walking. "No!" she replies firmly. "Pumpkins have orange flesh and have bumps all over their skin. I don't even like them. How about you try to use your infinite creativity and find another cute nickname for me. Maybe we can find an

American name for me to use. Many people do that here you know," she continues. "I like your real name," Andrew responds. "It rolls off my tongue so easily." "Thank you. I appreciate the compliment. So, just for today, let's take the stairs and side exit outside so you are not seen." She stops him for a minute and puts a warm stocking hat and sunglasses on him, adjusting them to her liking. "There, that's perfect! You're my secret agent man now!" she says with a big grin. "I'll be anything you want - besides that," Andrew replies, "I've played secret agent man long enough to know I don't like it." Ji-woo laughs and holds Andrew's hand as they race down the ten flights of stairs.

Once outside, they make their way down the street for several blocks to the subway station entrance. Andrew had passed by this station entrance many times without ever having the option to use it. "It's OK," she tells him as she pulls him with her down the stairs to the underground subway terminal. They pause in front of a large area map as Ji-woo points out to Andrew where they are now and where the train will be taking them. She walks up to a ticket kiosk and buys two tickets. She turns and shows them to Andrew saying, "Two tickets to paradise." They both smile and head through the turnstile eventually making their way to the outbound terminal. The train arrives in only minutes and they make their way onto it. Ji-woo leads them to a cozy seating area for two. They sit next to one another with Andrew's arm over her shoulder and her head resting on his chest. "This is a long ride and I usually fall asleep but I think I'm too excited to have that happen tonight. We take this train to the very last stop," Ji-woo mentions. They cuddle up even closer to each other as Andrew replies, "Try to get some rest if you can. I'll be here holding you the whole time. Besides, I have so much adrenaline running through me right now that it will be impossible for me to sleep." She smiles and taps Andrew's chest gently as if gesturing to settle him down. Ji-woo tries to resist falling asleep but soon her heavy eyes slowly close in the comfort of Andrew's embrace.

When the train finally reaches the last stop, Andrew kisses Ji-woo on her forehead until she wakes up. "I think we're here," reports Andrew. Ji-woo looks around and sees that they are the last ones on the train. She also looks out at the station name and says, "You're right. Let's go." They make their way out of the station and Ji-woo leads them towards a car that has its engine running and the headlights on. As they approach, the car door opens and a young woman gets out and runs quickly toward Ji-woo and hugs her tightly. They speak in Korean briefly and Ji-woo turns to Andrew. Both women are staring at him as Ji-woo says, "This is my friend, Andrew. Andrew, this is my sister, Mee-yon. She will drive us the rest of the way home." Andrew takes Mee-yon's hand, bows gently and says, "It's a pleasure to meet you. Thank you for coming out to pick us up at such a late hour." "I would do anything for my big sister," Mee-yon replies. They all hop in the car and pull away from the station. "I've heard so much about you that I feel I already know you. Your music is very beautiful and it has become very popular everywhere. You are now a celebrity. We are very happy that you and Ji-woo have come to visit. Our parents are also very excited to meet you," Mee-yon continues. "Please relax and breathe or you will pass out from non-stop talking, Mee-yon!" Ji-woo remarks. "My sister will ask you five hundred questions before our trip is over if we let her," Ji-woo warns Andrew and softly laughs. Mee-yon turns to Ji-woo and gives her a look of displeasure stating, "You'll pay for that." Ji-woo displays a big grin as she looks back at Andrew who is sitting in the back seat. As Andrew peers out the window, Ji-woo tells him that the landscape is hard to see at night and he will really appreciate its beauty in the morning when he is able to see. "Our parents' home is high on the side of a mountain and overlooks a great valley. You will really like the view," Mee-yon states and continues, "You'll also appreciate this old car of mine and the fact that we are not hiking our way up the mountain side."

Ji-woo apologizes to Andrew in advance and says that she would like to speak with her sister in Korean. "I don't mind at all," replies Andrew. The two girls speak for about ten minutes or so. Mee-yon appears to quiet down afterwards. "Is everything alright?" inquires Andrew. "I just explained to my sister that I don't mind that she borrows all of my clothes and things, but you are off limits to her," Ji-woo replies. "She must really like you Andrew! She is never jealous like this. From everything she has told me about you, I can't blame her," Mee-yon adds and concludes, "It will be hard for me not to tease my sister when I have been doing it very successfully all my life." This time it is Ji-woo who turns to her sister with a look of displeasure while Mee-yon laughs out loud. Although Andrew is quite amused, he has the good sense to stay out of the sibling conflict and just smiles.

All the conversation has made time pass quickly. Mee-yon pulls down a small road and approaches a home that is dimly lit from within and at the same time is warmly inviting. "We are here," she announces. "My parents only speak Korean so I will translate for you. Fortunately for us, they are sleeping now so you do not have to face five hundred questions from them this evening," Ji-woo says and softly laughs. The couple collect their things from the car and the three of them make their way through the darkness to the front door. Andrew remarks at how beautiful and bright the stars are tonight. "There are no city lights out here so the stars are bright and clear enough to reach out and grab them. My sister and I used to lie outside at night and pick out our favorite stars and name them. I know where all my stars are to this day. You are the brightest star right now, Andrew. I can see the twinkle in Ji-woo's eyes," Mee-yon comments with a big smile.

Once Andrew enters the home along with the girls, he marvels at the home's interior design. It is simple but elegant and has a sense of serenity. Ji-woo tells Andrew, "You can see everything better in the morning. I will take you to my old bedroom where you can sleep." "Alone!" Mee-yon blurts out while softly laughing. Ji-woo points to Mee-yon's bedroom continuously until Mee-yon gets the hint and leaves the couple behind. Ji-woo then shows Andrew to her room and pulls down the sheets for him on her bed. "My parents are old fashioned so I will be sleeping in my sister's room. I hope you understand." "No problem. I'll just gaze out the window and try to guess which stars belong to you." Ji-woo has a big smile on her face as she pulls Andrew close to her and kisses him goodnight. As Andrew sits back on the bed and looks around the room, he notices how very different the interior design is as compared to a typical American home. The beds are low to the floor and the walls are wood framed with thin walled rice paper on the interior walls that separate the rooms. The outside walls are thicker and insulated of course, but everything inside the space is either natural wood or white surfaces. The room is quite comfortable and pleasing to the senses. Andrew sheds his clothes and lays back in bed where a sense of peace fills his being. This is only occasionally disturbed by the sounds of the two girls talking to each other and giggling like children from the other room. He ventures to guess that they will not be getting much sleep carrying on like they are. He, on the other hand, is exhausted and falls asleep while staring at the stars from Ji-woo's pillow.

The rising sun shines down on Ji-woo's face as she wakes up, gets dressed and sneaks into her room where she suspects that Andrew is still sleeping. She opens the door and panics when she finds the bed empty and neatly made. "Where is he?" she says to herself in an alarming tone. She runs to the window to find Andrew standing on a precipice overlooking the deep valley below and the mountains reaching the heavens directly across the valley. Her father is standing beside Andrew with his outreaching arm pointing out various areas on the horizon. Ji-woo is immediately relieved and heads to the kitchen where her mother is preparing breakfast. "Good morning Um Ma (mother)," Ji-woo says to her mother in Korean and continues, "Have you met Andrew?" "Yes, I have Ji-woo. He has all of my favorite attributes; he's tall, dark and handsome!" her mother replies and asks, "Do you like him?" "I like him a lot, Um Ma. He is very different and nothing like I would expect from an American. He makes me feel very special," Ji-woo replies. "I can see it in your eyes my child that you are very happy. We want only the best for you. Although I would like to see you with a nice

Korean boy, I can tell that Andrew has a kind heart and after everything he's been through, I also know that he has a very strong will. Your father is already fond of him after everything that Mee-yon has told us about Andrew's struggles and triumphs. Look at them both outside there in the garden. Neither one can understand a single word the other is saying, but that does not stop them. Only men can do that!" Ji-woo's mother exclaims. Ji-woo hugs her mother and kisses her. She then prepares several cups of hot tea and makes her way out to join the men in the garden.

"Good morning Andrew. Good morning Ah-bo-jee (father)," Ji-woo says softly. "Would you like some hot tea?" "Gamsahabnida (thank you) Ji-woo," responds Andrew. Both Ji-woo and her father laugh in amazement at Andrew's attempt at speaking Korean. Ji-woo asks, "Where did you learn that?" "That's the only word I know. I went down to the front desk at the hotel and asked them to teach me how to say 'thank you.' I rehearsed it for hours. I just want people to know that I am at least trying," Andrew replies. "Well take your time learning. I like being your interpreter; it makes me feel needed," she responds. Ji-woo's father gently puts his hand on the side of her face and caresses it telling her, "I like him," in Korean. He then bows to Andrew and leaves the couple alone in the garden as he slowly makes his way back to the house. He can be heard in the distance saying "gamsahabnida" to himself several times and laughing.

"You've made a big impression on my parents," Ji-woo states and continues, "I have never seen my father bow and show respect to an American before. He must really like you." "I think they are adorable. Now I see where you get it from," Andrew replies. They sit in the garden looking out at the landscape and sipping their tea. "I love it here!" Andrew says with conviction and continues, "You were right about this being paradise. I don't know how anyone could leave this place." "I work in the city only to make enough money to keep my parents here and buy a few things for myself. You would never find me in the city otherwise. I grew up here. You can see the sun rise on one side of the mountain and walk to the other side to see the sun set. I guess I'm a real country girl," Ji-woo replies. Together, holding their tea cups and each other, they tour the gardens and Ji-woo points out the village center down in the valley visible in the distance. "We will go there today and visit. You will like it. The streets are very small and filled with shops and some of my favorite restaurants," Ji woo tells Andrew. He smiles and nods his head in approval.

They return to the house and sit down for breakfast with the family including Mee-yon who is joking that Ji-woo kept her up all night. Ji-woo mildly states that it was Mee-yon who had a never-ending line of questioning. Breakfast is already laid out on the table and consists of various meat, rice and vegetable dishes along with bowls of steaming soup. "I'm sorry we don't have corn flakes or a breakfast dripping with bacon fat you are probably used to in America, but this is a very traditional breakfast for us. In any case I'm sure you will find it is better than the hotel buffet," Ji-woo comments. Her parents are quite amused at Andrew's skill with chopsticks. They watch him, smiling and commenting to each other in Korean. In fact, most of the conversation at the table is in Korean and Ji-woo interprets anything meaningful for Andrew but purposely leaves out any comments meant to embarrass her in front of him. Mee-yon is all too anxious to fill in the gaps for Andrew. Andrew is convinced Ji-woo actually kicks Mee-yon under the table several times to send her a message.

Andrew gets up from the table when he is done and says, "Gamsahabnida." Everyone at the table laughs as Ji-woo comments, "You are making a lot of headway with that one word." She announces to the family that she and Andrew will be going into the village for the day. Before Mee-yon can get a word out and invite herself, Ji-woo turns to her and tells her that this is a private tour. The look on Mee-yon's face speaks volumes but she manages, with some effort, to smile and brings her dishes to the sink. Ji-woo asks Andrew if he could manage the hike back up the mountain from the village when they are ready to return. Andrew replies, "If you can do it, I can do it also." These are words he will later regret. Ji-woo packs some water and a few snacks in a backpack and they head off down the dirt road turning and twisting its way to the village center. It's a beautiful sunny day and there is a gentle breeze moving the trees about. It appears to Andrew that the trees themselves are bowing as they pass and he smiles at the thought of this.

Once they reach the village, Andrew remarks at how small and narrow the streets actually are. They are also filled with people casually walking around carrying bags and shopping. There are lots of small open-air markets with local produce and artists displaying their work. The couple walk arm in arm covering the entire village over the course of the afternoon. Ji-woo asks Andrew if he is hungry and he replies, "After all of this walking around, yes, I think I am hungry enough to eat now if you are." She brings him to an old restaurant that she indicates has been around since she was a child. As they go inside and find an empty table, Ji-woo calls out to the waitress, "Yuh gkee yoh!" Andrew inquires, "Is that her name?" Ji-woo laughs out loud and says, "I hope not for her sake. It means 'come here.' They will leave us alone until we call out to them. I know it's different for you in restaurants back home." Ji-woo asks Andrew if he has ever tried abalone and he replies that he saw them crawling around in a tank but he couldn't get himself to try them. "Abalone is very delicious and you will love it, I promise. I will order some along with some other things so you can try it." After the waitress takes their food order in Korean, she brings back small dishes of various appetizers which Ji-woo explains to Andrews as they eat. Finally a sizzling cast iron plate of abalone is brought to the table. "It smells really good!" Andrew exclaims. "It tastes even better," Ji-woo replies as she picks up a slice of abalone with a thin slice of white vegetable and baked garlic and holds it up to Andrew's mouth saying, "Open wide." He takes the portion into his mouth and begins to chew it. With a surprised look on his face, he nods repeatedly as he finishes his first mouthful saying, "That is fantastic! I never expected it to be that good. It tastes almost like sea scallops back home." They both share the mounded plate of abalone which is completely filling. Andrew later cleans out one of the empty abalone shells and puts it up to the sunlight seeing the amazing reflective colors emanating out of the shell interior. "It's amazing how bumpy and ugly the outside of this shell is compared with the kaleidoscopic wonder hiding on the inside. It's simply beautiful," Andrew remarks.

When they are done with dinner, Andrew admits that he is embarrassed at not being able to pay the bill. "There are so many things I saw in the markets that I would like to buy for you but my credit cards, passport and ID have all been taken from me and I have almost run completely out of Korean won," he says with a look of disappointment. "All I want is to share my time with you Andrew," Ji-woo responds pulling him close to her and looking up into his eyes. "That is my treasure. Come, it's a long uphill climb home. That's the story of my life, ironically," she adds. Andrew puts his arm around Ji-woo's shoulder and they walk at a relaxed pace back through the village. He is so enamored by the quaintness of the small village that he wants to take it all in and form a solid memory of it if, by chance, he is never able to see it again. Ji-woo was right about the walk home. Andrew really believed he was in shape with all of the city walking he did, but this return trip bordered on mountain climbing. After certain areas with very steep grades, Ji-woo suggests that they stop and find a place to sit and rest. She declares that she is tired and needs a break to catch her breath, but Andrew knows better. She doesn't need to stop at all and it is he who needs the rest. In fact, she times the breaks based on Andrew's heavy breathing peaks. "This would take some getting used to," Andrew reluctantly admits. Ji-woo laughs out loud knowing how hard that was for Andrew to admit. "We are making progress on many levels," she replies while still laughing and holding her hand out to help Andrew up. They make it back to her parents' house and she is able to convince Andrew to make the added trip to the other side of the mountain in order to watch the sunset. There is a flat overlook with a thick cut wood bench that must be hundreds of years old by the looks of it. They rest there and talk as the sun sinks slowly behind the distant mountains. The view is breathtaking and watching it with Ji-woo in his arms is another memory he wants burned into his mind. The soft glow of the sun shining on Ji-woo's smiling face is better appreciated by Andrew than any painting or masterpiece he has ever seen in his life.

After the sun is completely hidden from sight, they get up and walk back to the house. On the way, Andrew asks Ji-woo if there is any possibility of them visiting a temple. "Of course we can. I'm sorry we did not do it sooner. There is a temple in the mountains not far from here. We will go there tomorrow. It is too far to walk so we will take the car," Ji-woo replies. Andrew jokingly states, "But I was looking forward to climbing up and down the mountain again." They both laugh at his obvious ridiculous comment. "Tell me if you still feel that way in the morning," she replies while choking from laughing so hard. Once back at the house, the entire family gathers for a light meal and then retire to the living room for tea and conversation. Ji-woo's father has the TV turned on since he was the first to sit down on the couch. Once everyone is seated, Mee-yon asks her father to change the TV station from baseball to the local news station. As they continue speaking in Korean with Ji-woo translating for Andrew, the news reporter announces breaking news. Andrew's picture is displayed on the TV screen making him instantly feel sick to his stomach. He does not understand the news reporter speaking in Korean so he tugs on Ji-woo's shirt as a reminder. She, like everyone else in the room, is fixated on the news report but she instantly begins to translate what is being said.

"There is now evidence that the American pictured here, Andrew Trainor, is innocent of the crimes he has been accused of. This station has learned of a plot that has been uncovered involving a member of our own intelligence agency in collusion with and paid for by an American firm to frame Mr. Trainor and detain him here in Seoul. The reasoning behind this corruption and its impact on an innocent man is still unclear. What is clear however it that this man is the victim of an unjust action. We contacted both the American firm and the national intelligence office for statements and both declined to comment. Mr. Trainor is also a musician and this station has learned that he has been composing music that is currently on the Internet and has reportedly gone viral. It is said that his music is inspired by our own Korean language and something that only he can see in it. We will continue to monitor this story and report any updates as they come into our studio."

There is a silence in the room for a brief moment followed by Ji-woo's father standing up and applauding. The rest of the family join him and congratulate Andrew one at a time with handshakes, joyful hugs and kisses. Andrew is overcome with emotion but does his best to retain his composure. Both he and Ji-woo have tears in their eyes as they hug each other tightly. Technically Andrew is still under detention but this is absolutely about to change. In fact their lives are about to change dramatically. Ji-woo apologizes to her family but explains to them that she and Andrew will need a little time alone to allow this news to sink in, so she wants to take him out for a walk in the garden. Ji-woo's mother replies that everyone understands and encourages them to take their time also saying, "I will bring you out some hot tea. We will have some sweet cakes and celebrate when you get back inside." "Thank you Um Ma," Ji-woo replies.

The couple walk arm in arm out to the hillside garden and sit on a bench overlooking the valley. It's almost completely dark so Ji-woo has brought a flashlight to light the path for them. She turns out the light and they both look up to the sky filled almost to capacity with bright stars. "I told you earlier about an elder from Seoul that Ki Young introduced me to in the old temple. He told me that the truth was like the brightest star up there," Andrew says, pointing to the sky. "And that it was always there, even during the light of day when it appears hidden. He predicted that the truth would be known and I would be free with so much certainty that it was like he could see the future. Even now that I know he was right, I still find it hard to believe." Andrew brings his gaze down from the sky only to see the stars again reflecting in Ji-woo's eyes. "I am so happy for you right now. I love you so strongly. It's a love I have never known. The emotional path I am on with you goes only one way. There is no going back for me. If you decide to return to America, I pray that you will want me to come with you," Ji-woo replies while wiping persistent tears from her eyes. "I am convinced that going back home would only put us both in danger. Leaving you is unthinkable for me and out of the question. You are my bright star and my truth. I will have to find work here somehow so that we can stay together. What I mean to say is that I want to stay here and above all I want to stay here with you," Andrew says with absolute conviction, still looking into Ji-woo's eyes. The couple embrace with the force of colliding stars and hold each other so tightly that each can feel the other's heart beating in concert with their own.

Ji-woo's mother brings out some tea for her daughter and Andrew and invites them back into the house for a celebration. She speaks with Ji-woo translating for Andrew, "The sun must be blinding after being in the dark for so long. Still, it must feel comforting on your face when you look to it." She smiles at Andrew and Ji-woo with nods of affirmation as they both take one of her hands and head back into the house. Once everyone is seated at the table in the kitchen, Mee-yon explains that her father has poured everyone a small glass of munbaeju, a traditional alcoholic drink held in high regard in their country. It is only brought out and shared on special occasions. As he picks up his glass, Andrew looks down at the bottle and all of the small cakes and pastries laid out on the table. He holds his glass out to meet the waiting glasses in everyone's hands and they shout out in unison "Geonbae!!" This is the Korean equivalent of "cheers" and Andrew does not need translation. As he is still fighting back tears while looking around at the happy faces, he says, "Thank you. Gamsahabnida. Thank you very much!"

After everyone has had their fill, they retire to the living room where Ji-woo insists the TV remain off. The conversation is casual and mostly centers on Andrew's interest in what it was like to grow up in the village when everyone was young including Ji-woo's parents. Life was hard, of course, and lacked many of the luxuries people enjoy today. But they would not trade their past for anything. "We have managed to remain close as a family in a world that looks to pull people apart," Ji-woo's father explains in Korean. "We are blessed to have each other and are honored to have you here with us now." "I am highly honored by your warm welcome and generosity. Ji-woo is lucky to have such a beautiful family," Andrew responds. The conversation continues for a brief time and before Mee-yon has a chance to get too many more questions directed at Andrew, Ji-woo announces that it is time for bed. "Tomorrow we are going to the Beopheungsa temple. Andrew would like to look at some of the sacred writings they have there." "Oh you must let me come along," begs Mee-yon. "If Andrew is going there to look for music in the sacred texts, this is something I just have to see!" she continues. "OK, I don't think Andrew will mind and besides, you can drive," replies Ji-woo. "It's settled then. Good night everybody."

She walks Andrew to her bedroom and they hold each other in a long passionate kiss before she leaves him in her room closing the door behind her. Andrew lays back on the bed and begins to laugh softly upon hearing the girls talking with (but mostly talking over) each other from the other room. Between the newscast replaying repeatedly in his mind and the marathon talking event taking place in the next room, there is little chance he will be getting any sleep. He pulls the pillow up a little closer to the window and stares up at the stars while slowly thanking them one by one.

15. STAIRWAY TO HEAVEN

Everyone is up early the next morning and excited about the temple visit. Andrew insists that Ji-woo invite her mother and father but they decline saying that the long walk is a little too much for them now. After breakfast, the two girls and Andrew jump in the car and head off to Beopheungsa temple. "It was built around 650 AD and is one of five temples in our country said to be home to the Buddha's crystallized remains. The temple is surrounded by beautiful mountains and is very scenic," Ji-woo explains. She continues, "Every time I go there it is a very moving experience." As the conversation continues in the car, the time passes quickly and before they know it they are parking the car at the lower temple gates. While hiking up the path and various stairways on the grounds, they pass a very large set of stone sculpted pillars; one is an elephant and the other is a dragon. At the first pagoda-roof building, there is a visitor center. Andrew buys three candles and some rice used as offerings to the monks living at the temple. Together the three of them light the candles and place them among the already burning candles, adding to an eternal flame of sorts. "The flame from the burning of these candles never goes out. We will leave the rice on the altar top and briefly pray for grace to fill our hearts," Ji-woo instructs the group.

After they meditate, Ji-woo heads off to speak with one of the temple monks. She returns with the monk who greets Andrew with a warm smile and a bow of respect. He does not speak English but Ji-woo translates his conversation. "I will be happy to show you some of our oldest sacred writings. This is not typically allowed but as long as you do not touch them, we will make an exception for you. Your beautiful lady friend has explained to me that you find music in our writings. I can only imagine that you have divine guidance in your art and although I see these words differently than you do, they are still music to my ears. Come, let us go. May the Buddha inspire you with his words." The group makes their way continuously uphill passing through various meditation halls, admiring many paintings and sculptures. They walk into a small decorative building at the end of the path and are asked to sit on the floor in front of a book stand. The monk goes into a room and returns with white gloves on his hands and gingerly rests an aging book in front of them. He opens the book to a passage that has been bookmarked with a silk ribbon. Andrew studies the text with intense interest. When he appears to be ready to do something, a perplexing look comes over his face as he leans over to Ji-woo and admits that he forgot to take paper and pencils along. "I have my cell phone with me. We can use the camera and take pictures of what you want. I will ask permission," Ji-woo replies and turns to the monk to explain the situation. She also translates his response, "This is also not allowed, but you are doing holy work and I think the heavens will forgive us all."

After taking countless pictures, they thank the monk and roam around the rest of the temple grounds exploring the relics and enjoying the beautiful mountain scenery. They sit on the grass in the shade of a very old tree and eat some sliced pear fruit and other snacks they packed in the morning. After taking in everything there is to see and taking a bunch of photos of themselves for posterity, they head back to the car and drive back to the house. On the return trip Mee-yon cannot contain her excitement and begins firing off questions. "Did you see music in the holy words?" she inquires. "Yes, I did and I just knew that I would," Andrew replies. "What is it like?" Ji-woo and Mee-yon ask simultaneously, virtually bouncing in their seats like children as Mee-yon finds it difficult to keep her eyes on the road. "Well, making music from the text is a process, but I can tell from the arrangement of the musical notes I saw that there is very beautiful music there just waiting to be revealed." Both Ji-woo and Mee-yon beg Andrew to go through his musical process back at the house. "We want to see first-hand how this works. If it's not too much trouble, can you write a song and can we watch you?" Ji-woo asks. "Well, I have no violin or piano. They are back at the hotel," Andrew laments. "I have a guitar!" Mee-yon blurts out with excitement. "I tried to learn to play it years ago but I am not very good. Can you play the guitar Andrew?" Mee-yon asks. "Yes, I play that too," Andrew replies. "Oh my God! I can't believe we are going to witness this!" Mee-yon exclaims, unable to contain her excitement. Ji-woo admits she is excited too but demands that Mee-yon stop speeding or the only music that will be playing will be at their funeral.

Back at the house, Andrew tells Ji-woo that he needs to get the pictures they took on paper or write them down somehow. She tells him that she can print them out from her phone on her computer. Together they review all the pictures they took and he asks her to print almost all of them. He will work with one now but will have the rest to bring back to the hotel. She races away with her phone and later comes back with a pile of printed pages. Mee-yon, in the meantime, has explained to her parents the events of the day and that Andrew is planning to write a song right in front of them. "We will see his magic with our own eyes!" she exclaims in Korean. After her conversation, she runs to her room and pulls her guitar out of the closet, wiping the dust off of it as she returns to the living room. She hands it to Andrew telling him that it might be out of tune. He picks at the strings and tunes them fairly quickly by ear. After impressing everyone in the room with just some simple practicing and warming up, he puts the guitar down and starts looking through the images from the scriptures. He settles on one page and puts the rest of the pile aside. He asks Ji-woo for a ruler and something to draw with. She races off and returns with the items. They all get up out of their seats and gather around Andrew as he makes music staff lines on the paper and then draws out the notes he sees in dark bold markings. You could hear a pin drop in the room as the group gazes first at the music Andrew is drawing and then up at his face. Andrew points out to everyone the finished musical notes and then picks up the guitar and plays them. "It does sound beautiful but where is the rest of the song?" Mee-yon asks.

Andrew explains that the first measure is found in the text, the second measure is the counterpoint to the first in a manner of speaking and he plays his interpretation of what he feels the second measure should be for them. He then stops playing and continues to explain that the third measure is a repeat of the first and replays it on the guitar again. He finally explains that the last measure of what is called the verse or the body of the song is partially like the second measure except it has to resolve itself or point back to the first note of the first verse. "It's easier for me to just show you," he says as he plays the verse out from beginning to end. Everyone is amazed. They clap and express how beautiful the song is. "Can you put words to this song?" asks Ji-woo. "I suppose I could," Andrew responds. He begins playing the first part of the song very slowly and hums along. He stops now and then to write down some thoughts he has experienced during the last two days at the house and in the village. As he starts putting some words to the music and begins to sing them out loud, the family is glued to his every move. He finally stops and apologizes to everyone, explaining that making music is a process and takes some time. He asks if he could take a break and work on the words since the music is the easy part right now. "Take your time, we will go make some tea," Ji-woo exclaims.

They leave Andrew in the room alone as they watch him from the kitchen and quietly speak about how talented he is. After a half hour or so, he calls out to Ji-woo and she brings him in some tea. The others return to the room also and sit down facing him. "Please remember that this is very rough but you will get the idea. The song is called *Something Strong to Hold*," Andrew explains. He then picks up the guitar and begins to play and sing an entire song complete with a chorus and multiple verses:

"On a trip through fields of gold we took the back roads cause they're old
There's more to life than driving cars since the highway takes you far
From where our roots have taken hold and where our family tales were told
There's more to life than chasing dreams that never end up like they seem

This old country's in our heart and it won't be torn apart
This here land is in our soul and gives us something strong to hold

We pulled aside to smell a rose and took a path to where it goes
And you just smiled along the way and weaved the beauty of the day
Life is not a great big house, fancy cars or all that stuff
Life is moments that are true, life is being here with you

This old country's in our heart and it won't be torn apart
This here land is in our soul and gives us something strong to hold

I've roamed this world from end to end and count the seconds until when
I find myself back here with you, what I was born here to do
I'll take your troubles and your strife and relieve them from your life
When there's nothing left to do, there is always me and you

This old country's in our heart and it won't be torn apart
This here land is in our soul and gives us something strong to hold
This old country's in our heart and it can't be torn apart
This here land is in our soul and gives us something strong to hold"

When Andrew finishes singing the song and puts down the guitar, he looks up to find an awestruck crowd in tears. Ji-woo's father stands up slowly and begins to clap. On cue, the others join him and move one at a time to hug Andrew. "I don't think I have ever heard something so beautiful," Ji-woo says with a trembling voice as she struggles to hold back her tears. Ji-woo's parents beg her to translate the words from the song to Korean so that they can understand them. She does so holding the lyrics in her hands which brings them to the brink of full out crying. Mee-yon bends over and picks up the scripture image Andrew wrote out the music notes on and says in amazement, "You got all of that from this?" Andrew nods in affirmation as he slowly picks up his tea. Ji-woo's mother walks up to Andrew once again and cradles his face in her hands. Looking and searching deeply into his eyes, she humbly says, "Gamsahabnida (thank you)." "Where did you come from? Are you sure you came from this planet?" Mee-yon asks. "In my opinion, he is out of this world. The better question is what are we going to do with you?" Ji-woo says out loud in a complimentary tone. "People need to hear your music. The most important question I have right now is, did you bring your recording boxes?" she asks Andrew. "Yes, I put them in my backpack just in case." "We need to get you to a quiet place and you need to record that song right away before you forget it," Ji-woo insists. "Please make me a copy of the tape," Mee-yon asks and continues, "I have a friend who works in the city at a recording studio. He will know what to do with it." Ji-woo and Andrew agree and they go off to record the song.

After they are done, she asks Andrew if he would like to continue playing or go out for a walk in the night air since this is their last night there and they will be returning to Seoul in the morning. He responds that he can play music anytime but he would prefer to go for a walk with her. "I would also like to say goodbye to your stars. I won't see them from the city," he says with a big grin. "Then we will just have to come back," Ji-woo responds with an equally big grin. They sit under the stars on some flat stones overlooking the darkened valley and chat for hours. "I don't want this night to ever end," she says softly as she looks Andrew straight in the eyes. "I don't want to go back to the city. I don't want to go back to work. I don't even want to leave your sight, but we have things we must do," Ji-woo laments. "Be brave for me. When I am finally out of the woods, I will be holding out my hands to greet you. Maybe we can come back here and just stay. We will have to see," Andrew replies.

They reluctantly return to the house and after a late dinner, they turn in for the night. Everyone is up early the next morning. The couple get their things together, eat a quick breakfast and Mee-yon prepares to drive them back to the train station. Ji-woo's parents make Andrew promise to return to see them again and after a round of hugs and kisses, they get in the car and drive off. Once at the train station, Mee-yon gives both Andrew and Ji-woo a big hug and tells Andrew on her way back to her car, "Don't let her keep you away from us too long!" Andrew laughs at her comment and the expression on Ji-woo's face. They hold onto one another and head into the station to get tickets for the ride back to Seoul. As they wait back outside for the train, a young mother and her very small child are playing. The young child is giggling and running around hiding behind trees and stone sculptures. When the mother finds her hiding daughter, the child laughs uncontrollably and runs off to hide again. Ji-woo and Andrew watch this with amusement. Ji-woo spontaneously asks Andrew if he likes children. "Of course I like children. I like you, don't I? And you are very childlike and innocent," he responds. Ji-woo punches Andrew on the shoulder just hard enough to let him know he's not as funny as he thinks. "I'm only a few years younger than you are and if I appear like a child, that's your fault. Being around you makes me let my guard down and want to have fun," Ji-woo responds. "We are both childlike and have been pushed unwillingly into adulthood," Andrew concludes. They continue their "childlike" conversation until the train is heard coming in the distance. "Come and take my hand little boy. I wouldn't want you to get lost," Ji-woo says to Andrew with a sly grin.

During the ride back to Seoul Ji-woo once again naps against Andrew's chest. Andrew, at peace and in love, calmly wonders how his situation has been evolving back in the big city.

16. THE RALLY CRY

The train pulls into the station in Seoul. "You'd better put your sunglasses and hat back on before we leave the station," Ji-woo suggests. "After that news cast you wouldn't want to attract a crowd." Andrew agrees that it's best and obliges her. They head up the stairs out of the station and onto the street level where they begin heading in the direction of the hotel. Ji-woo begins to notice that many people are heading in the same direction. In fact she soon realizes that not a single person is walking the other way. This strikes her as very odd and she leans over to tell Andrew that she believes something is wrong. Only moments later, as they turn the corner onto the main road leading to the hotel, the couple come to an immediate stop. There, in front of them, is a sea of people lining the sidewalks and the entire street in both directions leading up to and in front of Andrew's hotel. She instantly grabs Andrew by the hand and turns them around to walk in the opposite direction and back down the street they just came from. "What is it? Why do you think all those people are there?" Andrew asks. "They are there for you," she says in a matter of fact tone. "Do you really think so?" he responds. "Well maybe it's all the signs they are holding up with your name on it that gave me a clue," she replies with a smirk. "I've got to get you back inside the hotel without getting mobbed by the crowd. We will take the back way to the hotel and use the employee entrance. Don't let go of my hand!" she insists.

After winding through side streets and groups of people, Ji-woo finally makes it to the rear entrance of the hotel and races Andrew up the back stairs and into his room. She asks him to promise her that he will stay in his room and also stay away from the window. "Put on the TV," she says. "I'm going down to find out what is happening. I will be back. Please stay here and don't let anyone in." After exiting the elevator on the lobby floor, she sees another crowd of hotel employees and police gathered in a circular formation discussing something. She stops the first person who passes close enough to her and asks them what they know. "The news report combined with an Internet movement somehow got all these people to come here and protest on behalf of the American," the person explains. "They are demanding justice and his release. I've never seen anything like this." Ji-woo makes her way through the crowd only to be met by a blanket of faces as far as she can see on the streets outside. The hotel staff, under direction of the police officials, are taking a PA system out of one of the restaurants and setting it up in front of the people just outside the hotel. It appears they are planning to have someone address the crowd. Ji-woo can see news vans from all the major stations parked along the road and newscasters are interviewing various people in the street. The protest is peaceful but the sheer number of people has the authorities nervous.

Minutes after the hotel worker has the PA system turned on and tested, an old man walks up to the podium from the crowd. It is Jong-su from the temple and although Ji-woo has never met him, his reputation in Seoul precedes him. Without authority, he walks right up to the microphone and begins addressing the people. Ji-woo is already overwhelmed by the show of support from the staggering crowd and is unable to hold back the tears from her eyes; they are tears of joy. When Jung-su begins to speak, there is complete silence among the countless people. He begins: "We are a very old nation and a very good people. We cherish each other and admire the accomplishments of our neighbors. We honor, respect and pay homage to our ancestry and look to a bright future in the eyes of our children. Our children know the difference between right and wrong and so do we, although sometimes we choose to ignore it. What has happened to this innocent American is a tragedy and an embarrassment to us as a people. I have met this man myself and I can tell you with absolute conviction that in the face of the adversity we have thrust upon him, he has risen above it in a most honorable fashion. He is an inspiration to me and should be an inspiration to us all. On behalf of all of us standing here in support of this good man, I implore our elected officials to do the right thing and set this man free for he shall soar to new heights unimaginable to us."

Ji-woo has pulled the sleeve ends of her sweater up into her hands and is holding them up to her eyes trying to stop the stream of tears pouring down her face as she hears the roar of the crowd applauding and shouting out in support of Jong-su's sentiment. She becomes nervous about Andrew being in his room all alone and wants to go back to him now so she pulls herself together emotionally as she makes her way back through the people to the hotel lobby. As she gets off the elevator and walks down the hallway towards Andrew's door, she can hear people speaking. Now in total fear, she starts running towards his room and sees Andrew out in the hallway surrounded by police and officials in dark suits. She immediately charges towards the officials in front of Andrew, yelling at the top of her lungs in Korean, "Do not take him away!! Don't take him from me!! He's done nothing wrong!" As she plunges into two men with her arms extended like a battering ram, they block her and pull her aside to calm her down. They explain to her that Andrew is going to be set free. She is not convinced that she believes them.

She insists on accompanying Andrew wherever they are taking him and Andrew himself requests the same. They are taken to the same room Andrew was brought to after he first arrived and where he was accused of spying. Everyone sits down at the table and one of the officers comments that they are waiting for one more individual. Moments later a man, also dressed in a dark suit, walks in surrounded by several security men. Ji-woo whispers to Andrew that this man is the mayor of Seoul. "I would like to extend to you a formal apology on behalf of our government, Mr. Trainor. I just got off the phone with the national office of the presidency and this apology also comes from our highest authority. All of the charges and allegations against you are immediately dropped and you are now a free man. An official statement from our president exonerating you is being released to the media as we speak. Earlier today, a man we believe to be involved with this incident was placed under arrest pending an investigation. I have arranged for all of your personal belongings, passport and credit cards to be returned to you and you are free to stay here in Seoul at this hotel or any place of your choosing. We will cover your expenses in the interim. I would like to ask you if you would not mind accompanying me downstairs so that we might address this formidable crowd together," the mayor explains.

Andrew thanks the mayor and agrees to go with him outside. He holds on to Ji-woo with a strong grip as the group leaves the room and makes their way down the single flight of stairs to the front lobby. The mayor, his entourage and Andrew with Ji-woo in tow walk out the front door and gather around the podium in front of an anticipation-filled crowd. The mayor addresses the citizens in Korean as a quiet envelops the gathering.

"My fellow citizens, I stand before you with authorization from our distinguished president to declare that Mr. Andrew Trainor has been proven beyond question to be an innocent man." The crowd in unison cheers enthusiastically. "He was wrongly detained by corrupt elements within our ranks and we will find it very difficult to repair the damage that has been endured by this good man." The mayor now looks directly at Andrew and continues, "In a humble gesture on behalf of the Korean government, we would like to extend to you political asylum and invite you to remain here with us for as long as you wish. In particular, the music you are creating has taken our hearts and nation by storm and you have clearly established yourself as a national treasure. We can only hope that you choose to continue to find inspiration here among our people. Mr. Trainor, please accept our humble apologies. We are forever in your debt."

The mayor extends his hands to Andrew and they shake vigorously. Ji-woo thanks the mayor in Korean on Andrew's behalf and after Andrew bows in respect to a loud and cheering crowd, Ji-woo leads him directly back into the hotel and they return to his room. Andrew immediately notices that all of his confiscated personal belongings have been returned and placed on his room's office desk. The full impact of Andrew's freedom is now being fully realized by the couple. A sense of relief and profound happiness has taken hold but they are emotionally drained and cling to each other for mutual support. Everything has happened so quickly over the last few days and Andrew quietly savors the moments in Ji-woo's arms. Within fifteen minutes, Andrew has passed out from sheer exhaustion, yet Ji-woo is unable to sleep. All she can do is watch Andrew sleep as endless thoughts race through her head.

17. THE SWEET TASTE OF VICTORY

As Ji-woo lies next to Andrew, who is now in a deep sleep, a few things come to mind that she decides need to be acted upon right away. She gently gets out of bed without disturbing Andrew, grabs the bugged hotel key from the power saver slot in the room and heads down to the lobby. She hands the key back to the front desk staff and tells them with both conviction and a subdued grin that Andrew Trainor's hotel key no longer works and he would like a replacement. In fact, she demands two keys. The hotel staff of course know her personally so they smile knowingly at her and throw the old key in the garbage. As they hand Ji-woo two new keys, she asks them to hold all of his calls and messages for the remainder of the day.

Ji-woo then heads to the restaurant where she is scheduled to work for the evening. She asks to speak with her manager privately. Once seated in his office, she asks for the night off. Her manager, along with most of the people in the entire country, is fully aware of who Andrew is and the events of the day. It is also public knowledge that she is dating Andrew. With this in mind, the manager assures Ji-woo that he will have no problem getting her shift covered and offers to do anything else within his power to help the couple. This leads Ji-woo directly into her next request as she takes her manager up on his offer. She orders a dinner for two detailed down to the wine selection (the first red wine bottle Andrew requested of her when they met) and an assortment of sweet desserts. She asks that everything be brought up to the top floor bar lounge by 6 p.m., complete with table cloth, fine china and candle lighting. Ji-woo's manager smiles, nodding affirmatively, and he comments on how lucky she is and how lucky Andrew is to have her. She thanks him and lets him know that she is deeply grateful for his understanding.

Ji-woo walks back to the lobby and as she waits for the elevator to return to Andrew, her cell phone rings. She looks at the caller ID and answers the call. It is Mee-yon. "Is everything OK?" Please tell me what is happening. We all watched the events at the hotel on TV. Um Ma and Ah-bo-jee are overcome with happiness and Ah-bo-jee is still clapping. Please tell me everything!" Mee-yon begs her sister. Ji-woo explains everything that happened and also her plans to treat Andrew to a romantic dinner. Mee-yon tells Ji-woo that she has some very good news. "My friend brought the tape with Andrew's song into the recording studio where he works. After the studio owner and producer listened to it and saw the rally at the hotel on TV, he has decided to offer Andrew unlimited access to his studio including a recording engineering team and a wide variety of instruments. He would like to produce Andrew's songs, get them on the radio and get Andrew paid. He has asked to meet with Andrew as soon as possible. Ji-woo, the money they are talking about is very big; he will not have to do anything else for work. He can just focus on his music," Mee-yon says with obvious excitement. "I love you, Mee-yon! This is great news. Andrew will be so happy. I will tell him as soon as possible. Kiss Um Ma and Ah-bo-jee for me and I will call you again as soon as I can," Ji-woo replies.

Ji-woo hangs up the phone, holds it close to her heart and smiles with gratitude for the good fortune finally coming their way. She gets off the elevator and opens the door to Andrew's room. After placing the "Do Not Disturb" sign on the outside door handle and quietly closing the door behind her, she lays down next to the sleeping love of her life again. After a few hours of relaxing, she wakes Andrew up and asks him if he is getting hungry. "I've never been so hungry," he replies. "Great! If you want to wash up and get ready, I am treating you to dinner. Actually, dinner tonight is compliments of the hotel," Ji-woo says as she pulls Andrew up out of bed onto his feet.

As 6 p.m. approaches, the couple steps into the elevator and Ji-woo beats Andrew to the buttons. Instead of pressing the lobby button, she presses the button for the top floor as a perplexed Andrew looks on. "You know something I don't, Ji-woo?" "That is an understatement!" she responds with a huge smile on her face. They get off the elevator and are greeted by a hostess who shows them to their candlelit table with a panoramic view of the city and the river. The couple sit side by side as wine is served and a parade of appetizers begins to collect in front of them. Andrew recognizes the wine and smiles knowingly at Ji-woo holding up his wine glass for a toast. "Here's to you and me and what our future will be!" At the sound of clinking glasses, they sip the wine and look out at the setting sun dropping ever so slowly over a bridge straddling the river. The glow of the sun and the joy of the moment bring out a long sigh of relief from the couple. As they sit holding each other and enjoying the view, it's apparent to anyone who might be looking on that they are both deeply in love and in thought.

Ji-woo is holding herself back from blurting out the good news about the recording studio offer to Andrew as she makes up her mind that this news can wait just one more day. She does not want to spoil the moment they are sharing. At the very same time, Andrew has decided to ask Ji-woo to marry him and is planning out in his mind the sequence of events including asking her Ah-bo-jee for his daughter's hand in marriage and his ultimate proposal under the stars in the garden on the mountain. He decides to hold off on telling Ji-woo anything about it until the time is right. It can wait at least one more day, he thinks to himself as he looks deep into her eyes and they both return their gaze to the last moments of the setting sun.

18. SPECIAL DELIVERY

It is morning back in the offices of Tilton Global and a young man sits in an office staring at a mound of paperwork in front of him. He sighs and grabs a file folder from the top of the pile and opens it. Moments later, the office secretary enters the room holding a package. She hands him the package saying that it is addressed to the person holding his title. When she leaves the room, he studies the package before opening it. The label's return address is completely unrecognizable to him with the exception that the package was shipped from South Korea. He opens it to find a carefully wrapped small box. It is a handmade jewelry box made out of abalone and is incredibly detailed, showing signs of fine craftsmanship. The sunlight reflects a rainbow of kaleidoscopic colors onto the man's face and the surrounding room. He opens the box to find a small folded paper and a USB memory stick sitting on the deep jade green fabric that lines the box's interior. The note is written in Korean, so the man enters the characters into his translator application on his computer. After hitting the translate button, he sits back in his chair and stares at the message:

"Be careful what you wish for."

Made in the USA
Middletown, DE
21 October 2015